The Cowboy Christmas Distraction

Tiffany Noelle Chacon

WRITE HORSE
Publishing

Contents

To my family: for loving me, believing in me, and making it really, really hard to write dysfunctional families because of how nice you are.

The CCD Playlist

**THE COWBOY CHRISTMAS
DISTRACTION PLAYLIST:**

Scan the QR code or go
to the link below to listen
to some of the songs
mentioned in the book.

https://tinyurl.com/
ccdplaylist

Careful readers will discover

Something strange on the page.

If you take note you will uncover

A Christmas secret for any age.

Gen Z Schtick

"**Y**ou're fired."

These are the words coming out of Helen's mouth, my boss for the past year at Goldman Sachs. My mentor.

I hear them, but I don't.

At first, I think she must be joking. I lean back in the chair, crossing my arms as I bark out a laugh, but Helen's face is deathly still. I'm getting fired, no cap.

"I'm sorry, Mon."

Mon? This chick's going to call me by my nickname as she fires me? Helen's sitting behind her antique desk in her corner office with a view of Manhattan from two floor-to-ceiling windows, looking like the queen of Goldman Sachs. I'd say she's savage, but that's too much of a compliment right about now.

I take a deep breath, square my shoulders, and summon my inner girl boss. "But I'm the best analyst on your team," I say.

Helen nods, her old school lipstick shining from the bright over-head lights. "Probably the best one on the whole floor."

This enrages me. "Then why are you firing me if I'm so lit?" I'm feeling fiery, which means my "Miami voice," as my best friend Mila calls it, is coming out. It's a little bit Latina and a little bit hold-my-earrings while I throw down.

Helen gives me a sad smile. "In small part, this is why." She spreads her hands out to encompass *me*.

Of course she does. It's what everyone else does, too.

My voice is escalating to the brink of hysteria. "Because I'm a passionate Latin woman?" Every part of me wants to slam my hands down on the table, to get in her face—to unleash my inner Hialeah girl. South Bronx got nothing on us.

"Monica, you know full well that's not what I meant." I must've offended Helen because now she's calling me by my whole name. Next thing you know, she's going to pull out my double surname like my mother used to do when she was mad: *Monica Isabel Garcia Perez*. "We've had plenty of conversations about how difficult that kind of thinking makes our lives as women working in a man's world. Don't put words in my mouth."

"So then tell me why you're firing me." I click my nails together, a Lisa Kon shade of deep red spotted on Kendall Jenner last week.

"Well, the most pressing reason is because Ashton Smathers has filed a complaint with HR for sexual harassment."

I stand up, slamming my hands on the desk. Guess Hialeah girl can't be held back anymore. Sorry, not sorry. "What?!" Before I can stop myself, a string of curse words flies out of me. I'd like to assault Ashton Smathers the Fourth, but not sexually. Oh, no.

Ashton Smathers is everything that's wrong with the *bro* culture at Goldman. He's lazy, entitled, and thinks every woman should worship at his feet. Well, not *this* woman—and I made sure Ashton knew it. Any time we were teamed up for a project, I didn't let Ashton walk all over me and made sure our direct supervisor knew exactly who handled the work. I'll let you guess how Mr. Smathers felt about that.

"That little—"

Helen holds up a hand, cutting me off. "I know exactly what Smathers is like. Unfortunately, his dad's a senator. Very...involved in Ashton's success here."

"Of course he needs daddy to hold his hand, *ese man es mucho*—"

"Eh." Helen cuts me off again like an ill-timed buzzer before I curse Ashton Smathers in my native tongue. "I know, Monica, I know. But the thing is, he has evidence of you calling him a—" she mouths the words behind her hand like we're in third grade sharing a secret— "and it's incriminating enough that my boss is calling for your proverbial head. He doesn't want to get in hot water with Senator Smathers."

"I'm getting fired because I called him a few names? You know full well what kind of language goes on in the arena—" (our term for the analyst floor) "—and Smathers is the ring leader! He's the worst of all of them. I call him one innocent name one time—"

"Just once?" Helen's eyebrow raises, a smirk playing on her red lips.

I shrug. "Maybe like, once a day?" I study my nails for a moment. "Give or take a few."

Helen chuckles, shaking her head. "Monica."

"So you're just letting this happen?" I throw my hands up. "All that hype you spew about women supporting women and standing up for each other—"

"I have supported you at every turn, Monica." Helen stands, fixing me with her steely gray eyes. "Don't accuse me of something when you don't know what conversations are happening behind closed doors. I have stood up for you as far as I could. You are a stellar analyst, one of the best, but your whole..." She waves a hand at me. "Schtick makes people assume you can't be taken seriously."

I lean back, crossing my arms. "My *schtick*?"

"Yeah, you know, the whole GenZ thing you've got going on. It makes people think you're shallow and that they can't take you seriously."

"My looks shouldn't matter if I'm crushing at my job!"

"I agree, Mon, *of course* I do, but the reality is that it *does* matter. Especially because we unfortunately work with the Smathers of the world, in their den of lions, in fact." She waves a finger, encompassing the whole of Goldman Sachs.

I want to groan, to scream, even to cry—but not here, not now. I wish she'd waited till the end of the day to fire me; I don't want anyone to see me after this. But I won't lose it at Goldman, even in front of Helen. Who, prior to this, I'd considered a friend, even though she's so old.

"Look, I know this is terrible." She sits back in her chair, almost slumping in a way I've never seen her do. She's always straight-backed. "And the timing of it, before the holidays, is awful. But this is my challenge to you: show me you can change. Show me you can conduct yourself in a serious way and I will give you a glowing recommendation wherever you want to go next." She smiles at me, but I notice it doesn't quite reach her wrinkled eyes. Guess she hasn't been using the Hullu eye cream I gave her that's been trending on TikTok.

Whatever, her eye bags can wither away for all I care now.

She sighs deeply, as if she can hear my thoughts. "Otherwise, you're on your own and I'm afraid Smathers will make it increasingly difficult for you to find a job in the city."

"So, what, you want me to change the way I talk and cut my nails and you'll write me a recommendation letter or something?"

Helen sighs deeply yet again, rubbing her fingers over her eyelids, which is only contributing to her droopy eyelid problem. I've told her this many times. "I don't know what to tell you, Monica. All I can say is that change needs to happen. You need to take life more seriously and take yourself more seriously so that other people can invest in you. If you want a long-term commitment, you have to be commitment material." I wonder if she's talking about Goldman Sachs, or about my long list of "boy toys," as she calls them. She stands up and comes around the desk, holding her hands out to grasp my shoulders. "Look, I won't tell you what to do because I want to see a genuine change in you. Let's meet up after the holidays, okay? Don't be a stranger."

I mumble a goodbye, and she gives me an awkward hug before I leave her office. I head back to my workspace, where I refuse to pack up until everyone leaves because I will not let all these Goldman Sachs bros watch me exit.

Of all the things I expected to happen today, this was not one of them.

Helloooo, Distraction.

I make three phone calls the moment I leave Goldman Sachs—all to former colleagues or classmates who could possibly give me a job in the city ASAP. I get the same response from each one of them: *Sorry, I can't help you.*

I wonder if Daddy Smathers has already blacklisted me?

I wander the streets until snow flurries start falling. I check my weather app and find that a storm is on its way—not that that would keep New Yorkers off the streets, but still. I want to be home. Or, rather, at my apartment. I'm not sure where 'home' is right now—my parents' house in Miami never quite felt like a true home to me, which is why I opted to stay in the city for Christmas this year.

The wonderful and terrible thing about New York City is that you are literally one in nine million. You can lose yourself in the crowd without being truly alone. No one cares that I just got fired—it's a blessing and a curse. I don't want the humiliation of someone else knowing. But there's also a blunt reality that no one's going to stop to comfort the girl sobbing on the subway.

Ask me how I know.

I've got my AirPods in, listening to Olivia Rodrigo's "making the bed" as I ride the subway. I miss my stop and have to circle back, feeling like a zombie as I walk the underground tunnels.

My eyes are dry by the time I get back to the apartment I share with three other girls—a necessity despite my very respectable salary at Goldman Sachs. My *former* salary, I think with a grimace. I'll need to figure something out, stat. My lifestyle cannot be sustained for very long without a sizable income.

One of my roommates is already gone for the holidays, the other is a hermit and never leaves her room, but the third roommate, Elizabeth, is my spirit animal. She's already fitted out to party tonight, some exclusive thing at a rooftop bar in Manhattan. The thing about me and Elizabeth is that we're often judged for how we look, but it's just who we are: some people dress to the nines, but we break the scale. We dress to the elevens, minimum.

"Makeup's on fleek," I call to her as I hurry to my room—if I know Elizabeth, she'll notice that *my* makeup is ruined from an evening of tears. And I don't want to go there with her, or anyone.

Since I work with mostly bros at Goldman, Elizabeth's friends have become mine. We usually go out on Friday and Saturday nights, and sometimes grab brunch on Sundays. Most of them are waitresses trying to hit it big or consider themselves influencers, though they're micro-influencers at best.

I sit on the bathroom counter that I share with my roommate who's out of town, readying to fix my makeup before we go out. I don't want to go out—a storm is coming and it's going to be freezing, and I don't feel like partying right now—but I desperately need a distraction. A text from Mila comes through: *On our way to the airport! Can't wait to see you!*

She sends through a GIF of Jess and CeCe from New Girl celebrating. Mila and her husband, Alex, are coming up to visit along with an entourage of cowboys from their co-worker, Luke's, family. Apparently one of Luke's brothers is competing in the Professional Bull Riding event on Christmas Eve. So the whole family is coming up to watch and then have a snowy Christmas in the city, something they never get in Florida. Anya, Mila's sister, will join as well because she is dating Luke, and since Mila's family is from Ukraine and typically have a Christmas-style celebration on Three Kings Day in January, they are free to join the Craigs for a snowy Christmas in the city. And apparently Alex's mom is celebrating with her sister's family.

Personally, I was happy to have an excuse to ditch my family for Christmas and entertain Mila and Alex. They'll get in late tonight, and I have a whole weekend of holiday-themed NYC activities for us. The bull rider is tagging along, which is fine. I just hope he won't cramp my style.

I'll never understand these crazy horse people. My best friend Mila thinks it's entertaining to jump her fifteen-hundred-pound horse over obstacles that are taller than me. Sounds idiotic if you ask me. But bull riding? That's next-level stupid.

I send Mila back a GIF of a kid dancing, not my best GIF action ever, but I'm not exactly in the mood. I stare at my reflection, taking in the bags under my eyes from my stressful job and poor sleep hygiene. My undereye depuffer has long worn out since my morning application. I half-heartedly freshen up my makeup. It's something I normally geek out about—half the people I follow on TikTok are makeup artists—but tonight I can only muster a semi-perfect cat eye and bold lips. When I exit my room in a basic black bodycon dress and my basic makeup, Elizabeth gives me a once-over, clearly a question in her eyes, but doesn't say anything. I guess that's how deep our friendship is.

She's in a festive metallic dress with thigh-high boots and her blonde hair in a super slicked ponytail à la Ariana Grande. I'm in similar boots, and we debate if I should change so we're not too matchy-matchy. Not that anyone would ever accuse us of twinning—Elizabeth is model-tall with gray-blue eyes and a complexion straight from Scandinavia, whereas I'm short, curvy, with dark hair and eyes, and I can tan with the best of them. I'm the Selena Gomez to her Taylor Swift—even in my heeled boots, I only come up to Elizabeth's shoulder. Eventually we decide I can keep the boots on, and we don our coats, scarves and hats as well as our electric hand warmers.

Of course, Elizabeth's only aware of the storm because someone mentioned it on Snapchat. Not that I'm much better, but I check the weather app more than she does.

We leave the apartment, Elizabeth chatting about some kind of Christmas speakeasy where you have to know the secret phrase to get in. "Josh told me what it was, but he told Shella and Max too, so now I'm sure the entire borough knows about it. Not sure how epic it will be if everyone knows about it."

She glances at me, her blonde hair flipping with her movement, and I realize I'm supposed to respond to her. "If everyone knows about it, it's so not epic."

"Right? That's exactly what I said." She goes on chattering, leaving me to my thoughts. We meet up with Kimmy in front of the subway entrance and then the two of them are tittering about their nails and how Kimmy found out from Shella where Taylor Swift's nail lady works. And it's the first time I've really noticed what Helen was saying—this *is* shallow. It seems especially shallow while I feel like I'm drowning in my disappointment at being fired.

I may be a disaster when it comes to relationships with men, but I wasn't lying when I said I was lit at my job. Hella lit.

So to have that ripped away from me, I'm shook.

It's making me question everything. If I can't succeed at my job, what's the point of anything? I learned far too young that people leave, it's what they do. So I threw myself into my education, and then into Goldman Sachs, thinking foolishly that my job would never leave me. Guess I was wrong.

Makes me wonder what else I'm wrong about.

By the time we get to the indoor rooftop bar, I'm so over it. Elizabeth and Kimmy take off to get drinks, leaving me standing at the coat check. I know I need a distraction, to get out of my head, but this is *so* not speaking to me right now. I text Elizabeth, telling her that I got my period and I'm heading home.

Elizabeth: *oh nooo!!! I got stuff if you need??*

Me: *I have stuff, just bad cramps*

Elizabeth: *<GIF of sad puppy>*

Me: *<crying in shower GIF>*

We go back and forth sending each other GIFs, until Elizabeth drops off because I'm sure she's met a guy. I splurge on an Uber, even though I shouldn't be splurging on anything right now. I don't have a job. The reality hits me like I just got run over by the snowplow following right behind the Uber.

Back at my apartment, I change into comfy clothes—barely overcoming the desire to throw my thigh-high boots out of my third floor window. I climb into bed and start on a Netflix binge. Watching other people's problems always makes me feel better about mine.

I take out my makeup wipes, but decide not to use them—Mila will know for sure something's wrong if she shows up and I'm bare-faced.

I'm halfway through an episode of *Outer Banks* when Mila calls. I'll be honest, I want to forget she's coming up with her perfect husband and her perfect marriage and her perfect job. I don't exactly want to tell her I lost mine, and I'm like a wrecking ball to any semblance of a love life I might have.

I sit up and plaster on a smile, knowing Mila will be able to sense my mood even through the phone. "Milly Vanilly," I say in a sing-song voice.

"Hey Mon," she says with a sigh.

"What happened? Did your flight get in okay?"

"Well, first there was something wrong with the plane, and now that they've fixed that, they're saying there's a big storm up there and they canceled our flight." There's a crinkling sound on the other end, and I hear her say something to Alex and then she comes back on. "Sorry about that, we're trying to find a way home. I guess we'll try again in the morning but the airline's being super cagey about the whole thing. Apparently they're not responsible since it's an 'act of God' so they haven't been very accommodating."

"I'm so sorry, Mila. Sounds like a nightmare."

"It really has been."

"Just keep me updated with what happens tomorrow."

"Will do, but there's one other issue."

"Yeah?"

"Matthew Craig, you know, Luke's brother? He actually just landed in New York."

"Oh."

"Yeah, so is it okay if he still stays there even though we're not there?"

I hesitate, not wanting to host some random cowboy without Mila around. I don't even know the guy—having him sleep on my couch was one thing when I had the buffer of Mila and Alex.

Mila senses my hesitation and says, "I'm really sorry about this, Mon. He was coming in from Virginia and his flight made it before they shut things down. He's already at LaGuardia."

"And he can't get a hotel somewhere?" I know the Craig family has a rental house, but it's not theirs until Sunday, when the rest of the family is flying in.

Mila sighs. "He's cowboy-poor, unfortunately. He's the bull rider."

I groan. "Just my type."

"I could talk to Alex and see if we could pitch in—"

"No, no, it's okay. I'll put my big girl pants on and host the cow-boy." At least one of my roommates is still here and I won't be alone with this random cowdude.

"Thanks, bestie. You're a life saver."

"Oh don't worry, I'll let you make this up to me."

"I'm counting on it."

When we get off the phone, Mila already texted me and Cowboy Matthew together so I could share my address with him. I settle back into my show, drifting off under the covers until I hear a knock at the door. I stumble to the front, not even considering changing out of my pajama shorts and T-shirt.

When I open the door, I'm greeted, not by my idea of a cowboy, but with a capital-d Delicious tall drink of something *way* better than water. I'm talking venti vanilla bean Frappuccino, extra whip.

And I think: I've found my distraction.

The Cowboy

The cowboy tilts his head forward in greeting, and though he's missing a cowboy hat, I have the distinct feeling that he'd touch the rim of his hat if he were wearing one. His brilliant blue eyes remind me of this show on AppleTV called *Foundation*, where the inhabitants of a planet called Thespis have glowing blue eyes. There's a dusting of facial hair edging his tanned, chiseled face and his light brown hair is just a touch too long, curling at the tips.

Then I realize I've been standing here, devouring this poor cowboy with my eyes. I haven't even said anything.

"Uh, hi," I say eloquently.

"I'm looking for Monica," he says in a subtle Southern twang.

"I am me, I mean, that's me." Crushing it with the words, I am.

I open the door wider and gesture him into the apartment. "Sorry, I just woke up."

He nods, as if to say, *I can tell*, as he walks inside. The moment he's in, I realize just how tall this guy is. He makes our living room look like it's made for dolls instead of regular-sized humans.

"Is that all you have?" I gesture to his backpack, which has a cowboy hat dangling from it.

He nods. A man of many words, clearly. He keeps his eyes fixed on mine, not so much as straying for a moment down to my chest or legs, something I'm usually aware of with guys.

"I was planning to have you sleep on the couch," I say, stepping closer to him. "But you're a lot bigger than I thought." I flick my eyes at him flirtatiously, putting feelers out there for how much of a distraction this guy will be.

"This will be fine," he drawls as he tosses his backpack onto the couch without so much as a second glance at me. "Thanks for putting me up."

"Let me get you a pillow and blanket," I say, walking back toward my room. When I get to the doorway, I look over my shoulder to see if he's watched me leave.

He hasn't.

I know I'm still dressed in pajamas, but I'm slightly offended by the fact that this guy seems impervious to me. I'll just have to try harder, I guess.

I return with the pillow and blanket, getting closer to him than I absolutely need to, and I can sense him almost take a step back. "Do you need anything else?"

He glances around, still not looking at me anywhere but my eyes, and then with an almost-bashful look he says, "I'm starved."

I smile. "Of course you are." I put a hand on his arm and then say, "I'll get changed and we'll go grab something to eat."

"Oh, you don't need to do all that. I'll just take whatever you have here."

"Lucky for you, I have nothing here. But you're in New York City, Matthew. It's the best place to eat in the world."

He nods, not giving me so much as a twinge of a smile. What is *with* this guy?

"You think about what you want and I'll get changed. Give me a sec."

I rush back to my room and overthink my outfit for far too long. I go to change back into my dress and boots, but I get the sense that Cowboy Matthew wouldn't appreciate that as much as the average Joe. I almost pull out jeans and a flannel shirt I have from a cowboy-themed party I went to, but that feels too on the nose. I settle for an off-the-shoulder sweater and jeans with my thigh-high boots.

When I exit the room, the only response I get from Matthew is a slight widening of his eyes—it's not much, not what I'd normally strive for, but Matthew seems like a tough cookie to crack. I'll take whatever progress I can get.

It's not quite what I'd envisioned for a distraction when I first opened the front door and saw him there, but Matthew *is* proving to be a distraction, so I'm grateful.

For tonight, that's all I want. Distraction. Amnesia would be nice, but I'll settle for dissipation.

Matthew surprisingly chooses Japanese food and unsurprisingly dons his cowboy hat when we head to a restaurant close by. There's a lull in the storm, with only a few stray flurries falling.

"You sure they'll be open this late?" he asks. That's adorable. It's only nine PM.

"They don't call this the city that never sleeps for nothing," I say with a wink.

No reaction.

On our walk to the restaurant, I look for any excuse to touch Matthew. I put a hand on his arm as I point out notable places. At a crosswalk as we wait, I brush a snowflake off of his cheek. Then, I grab the nook of his arm and burrow into him when a blast of wind hits us.

All through this, Matthew is like a statue. He gives seemingly no response—only rigid acceptance of my touch. By the time we get to the restaurant, I'm concerned. I send Mila a quick text: *Is Matthew single??*

Mila: *Monica...*

Me: *just curious*

Mila: *he is single, but I don't think you're his type*

Me: *you know how I love a challenge*

Mila sends a GIF of someone shaking their head.

The Japanese restaurant is offering a festive saké flight, so I order us two flights with cranberry, apple cider and eggnog saké. I polish mine off before our dinner comes, but Matthew doesn't touch his, so I drink it for him. "What, are you a teetotaler?" I joke.

"Something like that," he says with a shrug.

"Oh my gosh, please tell me you're not one of those guys who doesn't drink because of your figure."

"My figure?"

I wave a hand at his chest. "You know, all the muscles and stuff."

My jaw almost drops when Matthew blushes. Have I ever seen a grown man blush? I'm not sure, but he totally does.

And that makes me rethink my whole strategy. Because here's a guy that won't ogle me, he doesn't drink, and he *blushes*. What kind of man is this? If we were playing Hot Guy Bingo, this combination of traits wouldn't come together if you filled up the whole board.

"It's not about that," he says. "It's more to do with my belief in God."

"God won't let you drink?"

He shakes his head. "It's more about the fact that I don't like who I am when I do drink."

"Hmm." I take another sip of my drink, eyebrow raised. An uptight cowboy who doesn't drink? What's a girl to do?

We make small talk as we eat our food, meanwhile the snowstorm outside has gotten a second wind. The juxtaposition between where we are, warm inside the restaurant, and the cold blizzard blowing through the streets of New York City, is stark.

I drain the last sip of Matthew's drink, slamming the glass back on the table. I lean forward, eyeing him. "So, how's a girl like me get a guy like you to loosen up?"

He leans onto his elbows, his eyes still steady and serious. There's not an ounce of playfulness here. "Who says a guy like me needs to loosen up?"

"Me. I do."

"For what purpose?"

"I don't know, to have fun?"

"I have plenty of fun."

"Really? Do tell."

He starts to tell me about his family's ranch, about riding horses and bulls. "Those eight seconds are when I feel most alive."

"So you're telling me that you have to feel like you're close to death in order to have fun?"

This gets a genuine laugh out of him, a short but sweet sound that fills the restaurant and makes me smile.

"What about dancing? Do you dance?" I ask him.

"Not typically."

"I think tonight's your night, cowboy." I gesture across the street, where a country line dancing bar is. That's the thing about New York City—there's something for everyone.

"That's alright, I'd rather turn in."

"Turn in to what? A pumpkin?" He doesn't laugh at that. "C'mon cowboy, I'm going dancing." I stand up from the table, giving him a flirtatious look over my shoulder. "You don't have to join if you don't want to."

He sighs, like I'm a deep inconvenience to him, rather than a beautiful, vibrant woman who wants his attention. He follows me toward the exit, opening the door for me. "After you," he says.

"Dancing?"

"If you wish."

And as excited as I am to go dancing with this hunk of a cowboy, I get the distinct feeling like he thinks he's babysitting me. Not exactly the vibe I'm going for.

After some line-dancing, which Matthew is decent at, I get some more drinks. An hour or so later, I'm getting closer to oblivion when Matthew cuts me off. "Time to go," he shouts over the music.

We grab our coats and step into a whiteout. We take our lives in our hands as we cross the street, but I've had enough alcohol tonight to not worry too much. Matthew throws an arm around me to keep me warm in the blizzard, and my plan solidifies. By the time we get to my place, my head is swimming happily with images of me and Matthew. Just for tonight.

Once the front door is closed, I whirl on him, pressing my body against his as I tug his head down toward mine. Except he doesn't budge, his lips don't meet mine, and all of the lovely thoughts I'd had earlier don't come to fruition.

"Whoa, whoa," he says, his hands on my shoulders, pulling me away from him.

"I thought, you and me," I wave a finger between us, but he shakes his head.

"That ain't—I'm not, it's not—" he stumbles over his words but I get the gist.

He doesn't want me.

I mean, what kind of saint like Matthew would want me, anyway? Who am I kidding?

"I get it." My face heats, the sting of rejection pumping fury through my veins. "You wouldn't be able to handle me anyway." I press my hands to his chest to push him away, but his hands close tighter around my shoulders, holding me in place.

"Let's get one thing straight," he says, his voice so low it's almost a growl. "My job involves staying on fifteen-hundred pounds of bull while they try to buck me off. If anyone can handle this—" he glances down at me, his eyes really taking me in for the first time, "It's me." His lips quirk, like he just told some kind of inside joke to himself. "And sweetheart, I may be a bull rider but my mama raised me to be a gentleman. And I don't take advantage of women, inebriated or otherwise. It's not my style."

My mind flits from thought to thought as I attempt to digest all that he said. I almost say, *I'm taking advantage of* you, *not the other way around, bull rider*. But I land on, "I'm not your sweetheart." And this time when I push, he lets me leave.

"Just get out of here," I say, balancing the press of emotions swirling in my chest. Sadness, anger, humiliation. I stalk to the fridge and fill a glass of water, suddenly needing the hydration. Matthew leans against the front door, crossing his arms, looking every inch the cowboy that he is.

"I ain't leaving," he says, watching me cautiously. "I'll give you your space, but I'll be here if you need me." And, as if he could read my mind, (*I did need you, and you turned me down!*) he clarifies, rubbing the back of his neck, "To hold back your hair or anything." He gestures at me, like he thinks I'm going to throw up after drinking tonight, and I scoff. Before he can offend me anymore, I whirl on my heels, wobbling precariously as I disappear into my bedroom.

I get ready for bed in a haze of fury—but if I'm being honest, the anger is more with myself than with Matthew. The words of JVKE's song "Angel Pt. 2" that I've been listening to on repeat lately. People like me really do break beautiful things. Beautiful things like Matthew.

But as I fall asleep, his words skip through my mind: *I ain't leaving, I ain't leaving.* I shouldn't care about some throwaway statement he made while he was rejecting me, but I do.

Because isn't that what I've always wanted: for someone to not leave me?

Why, Indeed.

Turns out, Cowboy Matthew was right to be concerned about me throwing up. First thing the next morning, I'm running to the bathroom with last night's saké burning my throat. I momentarily forget about the cowboy while my stomach is being emptied, until I feel him behind me, holding back my hair.

As sweet as the gesture is, I wish he wouldn't.

I don't trust people who do what they say—I can't afford to. Because one way or another, they'll let me down—and I'll do the same to them. And I know Matthew, my weekend distraction, will be no different.

Nonetheless, it's sweet as Matthew rubs my back and murmurs reassurances to me.

Is this guy for real?

I'll be honest, I've done my fair share of throwing up and I've never had a guy do this for me. And we didn't even hook up.

When I'm done throwing up, I relax into a heap on the ground of the bathroom. The floor is cool and feels good against my warm cheek. Matthew gets up and comes back a moment later with a glass of water. Then, he finds a washcloth, wets it and hands it to me. I wipe my face, waffling back and forth between feeling embarrassed and grateful.

"Thank you," I croak.

He nods—still a man of many words, apparently—and then helps me stand up. "Why don't you get cleaned up, and then you can tell me all you have planned for this weekend."

I look up at him, feeling suddenly very vulnerable and immensely tiny as his bulk fills up our small bathroom. "You still want to do stuff with me?"

He shrugs. "Mila mentioned you have a whole weekend planned. Why let that go to waste?"

Why, indeed. I lose myself for a moment in his watery blue eyes as he reaches out and tucks a strand of hair behind my ear, his fingertips lingering for a second on my neck. I take a step back, trying to snap myself out of it. Cowboy Matthew may be sweet, but at the end of the weekend he's leaving. He's a distraction, nothing more, nothing less. At least that's what I try to tell the annoying little butterflies swooping around in my stomach as I think about the way his fingertips felt on my neck.

Showers are their own small miracles. I step out of the bathroom feeling like a completely new person. What did people do before showers? I mean, seriously. How could one possibly recover from *anything* without that gloriously hot water beating down on them? Not to mention the wondrous powers of a heavenly body wash and scrub.

It doesn't seem like Elizabeth came home last night—not exactly unusual for her—but I send her a text to make sure she's alright. Our other roommate, Candice, sent me a text at three AM with a picture of Matthew on the couch, saying: *Didn't know the rodeo was in town.* Matthew's cowboy hat is resting on the arm of the couch right next to his head. I laugh at her message, reminding her that it's Mila's friend and that he is, in fact, a real, genuine cowboy.

I have a few texts from Mila saying they're at the Miami airport but are still having a hard time getting a flight. *It's a mad house here*, she says with a GIF of a cartoon dog in a burning house sitting at the table with a coffee mug saying "This is fine."

I grimace, knowing full well how chaotic MIA is on any given day—much less right before the holidays. I send back a GIF of Dumbledore saying "Good luck."

She's going to need it.

For today's outfit, I choose my super warm fleece-lined winter leggings and pair them with a plaid bodycon mini skirt. I layer on a cashmere sweater, scarf and cardigan underneath my heated down parka. The battery-operated parka was one of my first winter purchases when I moved to New York.

What can I say? Take the girl out of Florida, but can't take Florida out of the girl. My blood is thin, I need warmth.

I find Matthew in the living room wearing his cowboy hat and boots, looking like he just tumbled out of the wild, wild west. He and I leave the apartment and he indulges me in all of the activities I have planned for the morning. I tell myself that someone as angelic as Matthew deserves for me to not use him—to simply enjoy his company, and let him go at the end of the holiday without any heartache.

Though he's quiet, I find a hidden thrill in getting him to quirk a smile or give a rare chuckle. I appreciate that he lets me chatter on about this and that, but that he seems genuinely interested in what I'm saying. He's not zoning out.

Outside, the storm has passed—for now, anyway—and it's a winter wonderland. The crisp white snow is mostly untouched except for the freshly plowed streets. I love the way the snow clings to the trees, as if someone decorated each tree in the night just for Christmas.

At brunch at Sarabeth's, I strike gold when I get Matthew to start talking about his family. His eyes light up as he tells me about his saint of a mother—who raised four boys and one girl (who somehow survived having all those brothers!). He speaks of his father with respect bordering on reverence, teases his brothers even though they're not here to clap back, and tells me all about his sister Katie Jo, showing me videos of her trick riding. He scoots into the chair beside me to show me the videos, and I tell myself I'm not affected by his closeness. Guys don't usually have this kind of influence on me—typically, *I'm* the one doing the affecting, not the other way around.

"I'm beginning to think that you all have a few screws loose up there," I say, tapping his forehead, as we watch Katie Jo galloping around on her horse *hanging upside down*. It's unreal.

This gets a rare laugh out of him, which warms me. He turns his head, which is so close to mine, and smiles. "Watch this," he says, pointing back to the video. Katie Jo starts flipping around like she's a gymnast—and I suppose she is, just on horseback.

When our food arrives, my lemon and ricotta pancakes are the perfect blend of melt-in-your-mouth sweetness with just a hint of savory.

"*Vaya!* You *have* to try this," I say, holding up a bite of my breakfast. I don't even think about this—it's something I'd do with just about anyone—but as we sit there with my fork hovering in the air between us, I wonder if what I'm doing is inappropriate somehow. After what feels like an eternity, Matthew finally leans forward, taking the bite off my fork. I try not to watch him too closely—and fail. A guy shouldn't look so good eating food, it's just not fair.

He chews thoughtfully, nodding. "*Muy bien*," he says in the most gringo accent *ever*.

I laugh, covering my mouth with my hand. "Is the cowboy trying to speak Spanish?"

He shrugs, patches of pink gracing his cheeks. "I grew up in South Florida, I know a few words." His eyes flick to me, then back to his omelette, and I get the sense that Matthew's trying to make an effort with me. Maybe not a *romantic* effort, but a sweet sort of friendly attempt.

I take another bite of my pancakes, a flush of excitement as I realize his lips were just on the same fork that's touching mine.

I shake my head, wondering where the brazen Monica went. I think of Matthew's blush, and consider that maybe this angelic cowboy is a good influence on me.

Or, this is very, very bad.

I guess we'll just have to see.

Fully Functional Amygdala

After brunch, we walk to the Rockefeller Center and take pictures in front of the Christmas tree. "Such a cute couple," says the woman who takes our photo for us. Neither Matthew nor I correct her, and I find that I don't mind that she assumed it. He (adorably) sends the picture to his mom—and the fact that he openly admits it just makes it that much better.

I drag him to the Rock observation deck, but he's kicking and screaming the whole way. "Didn't you say you were a bull rider? You can't handle heights?"

"I still have a fully functional amygdala, despite my choice of job," he says with a little more sass than I've seen from him.

"Don't worry, Matthew," I whisper to him. "I'll hold your hand if you get scared," I say in a baby voice. He rolls his eyes, but when we get out to the deck, he takes my hand and keeps it in a death grip as we stroll through the deck. We take another picture, but he doesn't smile in this one. The poor guy is sweating by the time we get back in the elevator and I tease him to try to distract him.

"It's a good thing your little rodeo event isn't up here, hm?"

He gives a little grunt of acknowledgement, eyes barely open, as we ride the elevator down.

We walk to Bryant Park's winter village and browse the holiday vendors there. I help him pick out gifts for his mom and Katie Jo. "You don't get gifts for your brothers?" I ask.

He shakes his head. "Mama cut that off after our gifts, that were really just pranks, got a little out of hand." A brilliant smile spreads across his face. "We called it Prankmas. It was epic."

I raise an eyebrow, curious what 'out of hand' might look like for this group of straight-laced cowboys. "What's the craziest gift you got?"

He grimaces. "You don't want to know."

"Oh, but I really do."

He glances at me with a little smirk that makes my stupid stomach do a little flip.

He quickly changes the subject. "Wanna go for a spin?" Matthew gestures at the ice skating rink and I know he's trying to derail the Prankmas conversation—which only makes me that much more curious about what went down. "Ice skating, that seems really Christmassy."

I shake my head quickly. Going ice skating with Matthew sounds kind of wonderful—a little too wonderful, actually. Romantic, even. But ice skating was my thing with Eduardo—my first real boyfriend, the only guy I ever truly envisioned a future with. He was my figure skating instructor, which sounds so cliché, but there's a reason there's books and movies with that trope. You spend so much time together in close contact, if there's any underlying attraction, it's bound to lead somewhere eventually. And it did lead somewhere, until our relationship ran into a dead-end that looked like a cute blonde.

"Don't tell me you're scared," Matthew says, with a teasing twinkle in his eye. *Is he flirting with me*? I force myself back to the present, leaving Eduardo behind as I take note of the way Matthew's leaning in toward me, daring me to skate with him.

I snort, rolling my eyes. "Trust me, I'm not scared."

"Oh, really? Because it kind of sounds like..." he puts his hand around his ear, listening. Then, he starts making chicken noises out of the corner of his mouth.

I smack his arm. "Don't be a dork."

"Why?" He straightens, eyeing me curiously. "Wouldn't deign to hang with someone so uncool?"

It's a challenge, and I wonder if this is what he thinks of me—someone so obsessed with their image that I would only hang out with certain types of people. "I think you're cool."

"Really? Even though I don't drink and don't do random hookups?"

"Well, when you say it like that..." I turn on my heel and walk away, making it three steps until I turn back around to find Matthew staring at me agape. "I'm kidding, Matthew!" I grab his shoulder and give a little shake—forcing myself to let go once I notice the very defined muscles there. "I like that you have..." I trail off, thinking of how to define what, exactly, Matthew has. "Boundaries. You have strong boundaries. It's cool, in its own way."

He stares at me for a few beats, his eyes roaming my face, like he's trying to tell if I'm being serious. Then, he nods, takes my hand, and leads me toward the ice skating rink.

Once we've got our skates on, we glide onto the ice and Matthew says, "Let's see what you got, scaredy-cat."

I raise both eyebrows at this, then turn and skate into the center where there are less people. I warm up with some mohawk turns, then a forward spiral, and finish with a two-foot spin. I skate back to Matthew, who's holding on to the wall. "Very impressive," he says with a genuine grin.

"Alright, now it's your turn, cowboy."

He lets go of the wall, only to tumble forward into my arms, his feet flailing around him. "I see how it is," I tell him. "You just wanted an excuse for me to hold you, didn't you, Matthew?" I smirk at him, but he feels so good against me that it's hard to tease too much.

"I honestly thought this would be a little easier than it's turning out to be," he says as he tries—unsuccessfully—to get his feet under him.

"Maybe *you* should've been scared," I tease him.

"Maybe."

"Alright, grab onto my arms, let's get your balance." Matthew grabs hold of my forearms as I put my hands under his elbows to stabilize him. "Bend your knees a little, stay centered, there we go." I start skating backward, pulling Matthew with me, coaching him as I go.

Eventually, we're able to skate side-by-side, though Matthew still clings to my hand.

"What made you want to ice skate?" I ask him.

"Must be the holiday spirit," he says, as he lurches forward and I catch him, his cowboy hat flying off behind him. "Good thing I chose such a capable partner." He says with a small smile as he squeezes my hand, and my stomach drops because I'm quickly getting used to having Matthew beside me—for better or worse.

After we're done ice skating, Matthew announces he's hungry again. The guy must burn more calories than the Hulk, because he can throw down like no one I've ever seen—he's even got Mila beat, who can stuFf her face like a dude. And shockingly, I'd be hard pressed to find even five percent body fat on Matthew.

Not that I wouldn't mInd searching.

"You want to get the street vendor experience? Maybe a hot dog or a falafel?"

"I don't know what a falafel is, but a hot dog sounds good." He ends up ordering—and completely consuming—five hot dogs. As we eat, I notice how red Matthew's ears are.

"Matthew, you've got to be freezing. That hat isn't doiNg you any favors in the cold."

"Here I thought we were going for fashionable over functional," he says with a small lift of his lips. Matthew's making fun of me, I realize with utter delight.

I smack his arm, my hanD lingering a little longer than strictly necessary. "Hey, you can mock all you want but my down jacket has an electric heater installed in it."

"That seems...excessive."

"It's practical."

I dig in my purse, procuring a spare beanie, my electric hand warmer, and a fleece neck warmer. Mila always jokes about my purse being like a Mary Poppins bag, and she's not altogether incorrect. My Louis Vuitton Neverfull is aptly named.

I turn on the electric handwarmer. "Hands," I say, gesturing for him to hold out his hands. I take off his gloves, they're more of a leather worker's glove than for the cold. They're stiff from the cold, and clearly worn in certain places from prolonged use. I wrap his hands around the handwarmer and then place my hands around his, rubbing until I'm sure he's warmed up.

"Oh wow. What is this? Magic?"

"Something like that." I smile, peering up at him through my eyelashes. "You can hold it in your pocket and just switch back and forth between hands."

"Thanks, Monica."

I try to steady the beating of my heart at the sound of my name on lips. I've never appreciated a true Southern accent until right this moment.

"Alright now bend down, Mr. Bunyan," I tease. He tilts his head down and I take his cowboy hat, momentarily placing it on top of my slouchy hat. I tug the neck warmer over his head, and he laughs when I pull the edge of it over his nose and mouth. Then I place the beanie on his head, tucking it over his ears. I momentarily clasp my palms over his ears, trying to warm them.

"I think I'm starting to be able to feel the tips of my ears again," Matthew says, and I'm so aware of how close we are. His face is almost level with mine, and with my hands around his head like this, I could easily pull his mouth to mine.

Not that I would. I'm just saying, I *could*.

His eyes flick over mine, as if he just read my mind.

"Don't worry," I say in a low voice. "I won't accost you again." I run my hands over his shoulders, smoothing his jacket. "I get it now."

I pull away before my body revolts against my mind.

"This hat is like velvet," Matthew says as he straightens, running a hand over it.

"Right? It's from that company Barefoot Dreams. You know, the one with the blanket Chrissy Teigen loves?"

"Oh yeah, Chrissy Teigen, yeah, totally." He picks the cowboy hat off my head and places it back on his own with a smile.

I laugh at his tone, wondering if I can keep this playful version of Matthew.

We walk to Times Square and stand in the center while seemingly all of New York moves around us. I watch Matthew as he takes it all in. I expected him to be overwhelmed by the crowds and the chaos, but he takes it in stride, looking as calm as he usually does.

"Can I take your picture?" I ask. When he looks warily at me, I say, "For your mom?"

He sighs. "Low blow, Monica."

"I'm learning all of your weaknesses, Matthew."

I take a few steps back and start taking pictures of him. At first, he smiles. "Don't smile," I tell him. I capture several in portrait mode, where the lit-up buildings behind him are shining in their clarity, the people around him are slightly blurred, and he's the clearest thing in the photo. His eyes are slightly wary in their magnetic blue, his jaw clenching and unclenching, the muscle flicking. Curls of light brown hair escape from the side of the beanie. His hands are in fists in his jacket pockets.

Honestly, it looks like the cover of an album. He's gorgeous, and his eyes alone tell their own story—one I'm only starting to figure out.

"Perfect," I tell him. I'm about to grab his hand and pull him toward the subway when he says, "Your turn."

I'm comfortable in front of the camera, so I quickly make a few flirtatious faces while he clicks my phone camera. After a moment, he lowers the phone. "Just be you," he says. "The real Monica."

The real Monica? I don't even know what that means. But as I stand there in the middle of Manhattan, I slowly let my walls fall. And just let myself show through—whatever that means. I don't know what story *my* eyes will tell when I look at this picture, but when Matthew hands the phone back to me and mirrors my phrase, "perfect," I stuff the phone in my pocket, too scared to look.

Don't Catch Fratbro

We take the subway to my apartment, a comfortable silence stretching between us as we ride the underground.

When we're inside, Matthew calls his parents while I change into something a little nicer for us to head to the "secret" Christmas speakeasy.

I check in with Mila, who tells me that they couldn't get on a flight for today, but that they found one for tomorrow evening. I send her a bunch of GIFs—one of two baby bunnies snuggling that says '*besitos.*' I know how frustrating her holiday airport experience must be—I definitely wouldn't wish that on my worst enemy, much less my best friend.

On second thought, I'd *love* it if Ashton Smathers got stuck in a never-ending holiday nightmare in the Miami airport with crowds, rude airline employees, and canceled flights.

I hear Elizabeth in her room, and I should probably ask if she wants to come with us to the speakeasy. I know Elizabeth's leaving first thing tomorrow for her parents' house in Connecticut. I tell myself that she probably needs to pack, which is why I don't invite her to come with us. Though the truth is that I want Matthew all to myself.

We take the subway to Hell's Kitchen, and I follow the instructions Elizabeth's friend gave me. The first door we try is the wrong one, so we walk one more block and try again. This time, a gruff man in a too-small elf outfit opens the door, and he does *not* look happy.

"Whatd'ya want?" he snaps.

"The merriest Christmas ever?" I say the secret phrase hesitantly, because this elf looks like he's going to throw us back onto the street at any moment.

"Yeah, yeah, you're in the right spot," he says, ushering us inside. We climb down a flight of darkened stairs, past a forest of fake Christmas trees, and through another door.

That's when we enter Wonderland.

There are a series of rooms, and each one is equally incredible—and a little trippy, too.

In one room, everything is upside down. We walk over fluffs of cotton clouds, the floor glowing a sunny blue. Above us, Christmas trees are hanging upside from the ceiling. An animatronic bird flies—upside down—just above our heads.

In another room, it's like we're inside a snowglobe. There's clear plastic rounded walls with fake snow six inches deep. At the press of a button (that Matthew located), the globe "shakes"—which is more of just a rumbling sound coming through the speakers—and more snow starts to fall from the ceiling.

In another room, there's a Cirque du Soleil-style show with glittering aerialists spinning in silken ribbons from the ceiling.

Matthew and I pass from room to room in silent wonder, sometimes laughing or pointing out things to the other person, but generally just taking it in. It's a little like a haunted house, but opposite—you don't know what you'll get in each room, but it's a wonderful surprise.

As we walk through the rooms, I wonder what it would be like if Matthew were my boyfriend—not some random distraction or fling to fill the gaps of my life, but an actual permanent fixture in my life. I've never thought I was ready for that—I've never thought I was good enough for that, especially with someone like Matthew. But the past twenty-four hours has made me wonder.

The final room that we reach has a band playing contemporary takes on classic holiday music and there's a crowd at the bar. "You want a Coke or something?" I ask Matthew. He shakes his head, but then points at a steaming cup of hot chocolate with marshmallows floating on top. "I could go for something like that," he shouts over the music.

We press forward to the bar and try to get the bartender's attention. He meets our eye and then holds a finger up, telling us he'll be with us next. While we wait, we watch the band as they play a pop-version of Bing Crosby's "White Christmas."

That's when I see one of the guys who used to work with me at Goldman Sachs. His name is Austin, and not only was he relentlessly gross in his pursuit of me, but he wasn't even a good analyst, even though he got promoted before me. I almost grab Matthew's hand and dart out of here before Austin can spot me. But I'm not fast enough, because before I know it, Austin's right beside me, a boozy smile on his sleezy face.

"I heard you got the boot at Goldman," he says into my ear. When I don't respond, he leans in closer and says, "I've got a startup, would love to have you on board."

I think for a moment. I don't like Austin, not one bit. The way he ogled every female in sight and the things that would come out of his mouth...I've no interest in working for this King of Bros.

On the other hand, I need a job. Desperately. "Tell me more," I say. He gestures with his chin toward a corner of the room, where we won't have to yell to hear each other.

"I'll be right back," I tell Matthew, who eyes me warily.

Once we're at the edge of the room, Austin leans against the wall, beckoning me closer. I keep a modest distance, I don't want to catch *fratbro*—I've heard it's tough to get rid of.

"We're revolutionizing banking," he says. "Like BitCoin, but better. More innovative, yet more secure. I'm looking for analysts as we speak."

I ask him a few questions, genuinely interested in the technology, but I'm playing my cards close to my chest when he leans in.

"C'mon, Mon," he says, the edge of his mouth tilting up in a way that would probably make a common girl get all hot and bothered. But I'm not so common. "We'd have *fun*." The way he says *fun*, I know exactly what he means. And exactly what that means he thinks of *me*. This isn't him recruiting me because of my talent, but because of my body. He has the audacity to reach over and try to run a finger over my lip. I smack his hand away, fuming.

I think of Helen's challenge to me, about people taking me seriously.

And it hurts so much to see evidence that she's right, standing right in front of me looking like a clown.

"Tempting," I say dryly. "But I think I'll pass." I give him a good head-to-toe look, let him know that I've measured him and found him wanting. I'm going to walk away when he grabs my arm, painfully, jerking me back toward him.

"You don't have to work with me to have a little entertainment tonight."

"Leave me alone," I say, trying to push him away.

"Girls don't say no to me." He's in my face, his breath reeking of alcohol.

"Good thing I'm not a girl." I finally manage to yank my arm from his. "I'm a grown woman."

I'm feeling pretty confident after my declaration, ready to strut away in my sky-high Manolo Blahniks. But when I feel his hand around my waist, clutching at me in a drunken grasp, I look over my shoulder, searching for Matthew. But he's nowhere to be found.

Austin slurs something in my ear, a dirty phrase I can't even hear because I'm fumbling in my purse as discreetly as I can. A few months ago, Elizabeth bought us all self-defense stick pens—they're basically pointy objects used to get someone off of you without actually stabbing them. The moment my fingers graze against something hard and smooth, I whip it out of my purse and press it into his chest.

"Let go of me," I growl, digging the object into his pecs.

Only, it isn't my stabbing stick-pen. Of course it isn't.

It's a tampon. One that had been in my purse for so long it got out of the wrapper.

I'm mortified.

At this point, I have two choices: I can lean into it, or I can try to run away. And seeing as how I'm wearing my aforementioned Manolos, I'm leaning into it.

I decide to let it rip on the King of Bros. "You are a bully, Austin. And maybe you think you're trying to flex right now, intimidating a woman half your size, but you know what? One day you'll be alone. Balding and lonely, with only a failed startup to your name, flailing around like the underdeveloped flagellum that you are." I'm poking him with my tampon with every word and even in my Manolos, I'm standing on my tiptoe to get as far into this guy's face as I can get. "And you know where I'll be?"

"Where's that?" he sneers.

"As far away from you as possible." I take a step back, and his hand miraculously drops away. This emboldens me, so I decide to add, "And I won't be alone," I say, more to myself than to him. Because I've decided something in this moment: I may not feel like I deserve Matthew, but I don't deserve to be alone either.

With a flourish, I throw the tampon in his face and whirl away.

And, whose chest do I collide with? That's right, Matthew.

He's standing directly behind me, his arms crossed over his chest, the muscle in his jaw flicking angrily. He must be the reason Austin actually let go of me.

"Do we have a problem here?" Matthew asks, his voice an octave deeper than it's already baritone timber.

"Not with me, man," Austin says, holding up his hands and backing away.

"Let's just get out of here," I tell Matthew. His brilliant blue eyes search mine, like he's trying to figure out if he needs to beat this guy up or not. But eventually he nods, takes my hand, and we walk out of the speakeasy.

Once we're in the crisp night air, I let out a whoop. My limbs are shaking with the adrenaline of standing up to Austin. "That was nuts!" I shout, feeling exhilarated.

"Did you just accost that guy with a...tampon?" Matthew's looking at me, wide-eyed and so insanely handsome.

I nod, a huge smile on my face.

Then he lets out the biggest, loudest laugh I've ever heard. His voice booms through the night, infecting me until I'm giggling and teetering on my heels.

We laugh all the way to the subway, which is packed with people heading out for the holiday weekend. We have to squish together in a corner, which I am absolutely not complaining about.

"That was kind of amazing," Matthew laughs. "I've never seen anything like it before. You are one-of-a-kind, Monica Perez."

I flush at his words, preening under his praise. For the first time, I feel empowered to change. To be someone who can reveal who I really am—and be accepted for that. I'm beginning to believe, at least with Matthew, that I don't have to be the Monica with all the walls up—I can be the real Monica. Though, I'm not quite sure who that is anymore.

The God Who Never Leaves

Since we didn't get our hot chocolate at the speakeasy, we stop at the corner market and pick up supplies to make our own. The snow is lightly falling once more, coating us in tiny flakes that make us look like we're covered in fairy dust.

Back at my apartment, we get into a semi-heated debate about which Christmas movies count as "real" Christmas movies. Matthew grew up in a family that watched all the classics like A *Christmas Story* and *Miracle on 34th Street*, whereas I'm a fan of more modern movies like *Elf* or *Noelle*.

"So you only watch Christmas movies made before you were born?" I scoff.

"It's their timelessness that makes them classic."

"And *boring*."

"A storyline with depth can often be perceived as boring by some."

Ouch. His comment hits a little too close to home. *By some*, meaning the shallow ones. Meaning, *me*.

"How's this for a compromise," he says, "let's watch one of each. One classic, one modern."

"Deal." He holds out his mug of hot chocolate, and we cheers.

I text Elizabeth to see if she wants to join us—a cop-out, I know, I should just knock on her door like a regular human being—and cross my fingers that she doesn't.

She texts me twenty minutes later saying she's going to bed early so she can catch the first train, and I can't help but smile.

I've got Matthew all to myself for one more night.

I've fallen asleep halfway through *It's a Wonderful Life*—and who can blame me—when the power goes out. The TV turns off, and I snap awake. Funny how silence can be more potent sometimes than noise.

"What're we going to do?" Matthew whispers into the darkened apartment.

"Well," I say, my voice low, "we'll have to snuggle to stay warm, or else we'll probably die from the cold." I stretch out my legs, tucking my toes under his leg to make my point.

"Really?" Matthew swallows, his throat bobbing. I can't tell in the dark, but I'd be willing to bet he's blushing.

"No, not really. We'll be fine, they usually get the power back on really quickly around here. Besides, it could be worse." I think about how much worse it would be if Matthew weren't here with me. I'd be all alone right now. Even Elizabeth's asleep.

"Worse than fifteen degrees?" Matthew says incredulously.

"I mean, it doesn't happen often, but last year we got down to seven degrees. Chill, Florida boy," I say with a teasing wink that he probably can't really see.

"Aren't you a Florida girl?"

"Kind of, I'm originally from Colombia."

"Does it get cold there?"

"There are parts of the country that have higher elevation and get colder, but I'm from Barranquilla, where it's tropical. Florida is cold comparatively," I say with a laugh.

"How long did you live there?"

"I moved here when I was eight."

"Oh, so you lived there for a while. I thought you came when you were really little or something."

"My parents came here when I was three to get residency, then they sent for me once they were settled."

He's quiet for a moment, then says in an almost-whisper, "You lived for five years without your parents?"

I nod, staring up at the ceiling as I try to channel all of my emotion out of me. It's normally a lot easier to do that—but something about Matthew is making me feel vulnerable, as if my parents just left me in Colombia.

"Wow. I can't imagine. What was that like?"

I suck in my breath. In all my twenty-six years, no one has asked me this before. What was it like having my parents abandon me and then one day return and whisk me away to another country like nothing ever happened? I think about this for a moment, how to even respond. The O.G. Monica would laugh it off, make a joke, put walls up, and pretend like I'm impenetrable.

But if this weekend has taught me anything, it's that I'm not impenetrable. And I want to be real. Even if I'm not 'serious' like Helen challenged me to be, I can show people—*some* people—who I really am.

I exhale and say, "It was horrible."

He's silent, giving me space to continue, so I do.

"I was just old enough to realize that they were leaving, but not quite mature enough to connect all the dots. I didn't know they were coming back, and my aunt, who I stayed with, didn't do a great job of communicating about it. Maybe she didn't really know. And it's not like we had FaceTime or something to keep up. It's just, I woke up one morning and my parents were gone. It's like I was all of a sudden an orphan, but didn't have the space or even the reason to grieve."

"I'm so sorry."

I shrug, but the moment I do it, I realize I can't shrug this off. I've been trying—for twenty years, I've been attempting to brush this part of my story, my life, off. Hasn't exactly worked for me, has it? "When they finally came to get me, I barely remembered them. And then I was in a new country, with seemingly new parents, and I was expected to just assimilate. They'd gotten used to the States, but it was all new for me. And by the time I got here, they were pregnant with my brother. I'd been here less than three months when he was born. I was trying to find my footing and all of a sudden there's a screaming baby taking up everyone's time."

"That must've been hard."

"Yeah, my parents aren't the greatest communicators. They have other great qualities, but that is not one of them." I laugh, a bit caustically. "I used to have these nightmares that they would leave me in the middle of the night. I would go to bed fully dressed, my shoes lined up right next to my bed so that if I heard anything, I would pop up out of bed and be ready to go with them. I didn't want to get left again."

"Wow."

"Yeah." My thoughts drift to my childhood, coming to the States. "That's when I started skating. I think my parents wanted me to do something, to be busy with something other than worry. Back in Colombia, my mom had been obsessed with this American film that they dubbed and showed at our local theater called Cutting Edge. It was about a figure skater and this retired hockey player who becomes her partner and they fall in love. I think because of that movie, she felt like figure skating was this, like, really American sport or something. But honestly, I think they just liked it because it was time-consuming. I was skating all the time—before school, after school, doing camps during school breaks." I don't tell him about Eduardo, who became my skating instructor around the time I turned eighteen when I moved up to the senior division. He was twenty-five—seven years my senior. Now, as a twenty-six-year-old, I wonder what in the world Eduardo was doing dating someone so young? I was naïve enough to think he was my forever love, when all along I was probably just a silly fling for him before he settled down.

"I'm sorry they didn't make you feel more loved," Matthew says, bringing my thoughts back to the present. "You deserve better."

I lean my head back over the edge of the couch, letting my hair fall over the side. I run my hands through my hair, pulling at strands and then letting them fall back down, the motion soothing me.

I don't know what to make of what Matthew just said. It's true that my parents' actions made me feel unloved, though I would never have put it that way myself. They were trying to make a better life for me, so I've always tried to justify what they did. Did I deserve better? I'm not sure. But the fact that Matthew believes I do makes me feel some type of way I can't quite put my finger on.

Just then, I feel a warm hand clasp my ankle. Matthew. "Hey, you okay?"

I shake my head, then confess, "I'm not sure I've ever been okay."

His thumb presses into the arch of my foot, and I let out an inadvertent groan. "That feels good."

"We did a lot of walking today." He moves expertly over my feet, massaging all the sore spots.

"You're really good at that," I say it almost accusingly—*what other girl has taught you to give foot massages*? And I wonder when I started to get possessive over Matthew, and how it could happen so quickly.

"Ma always wanted us to give her foot massages."

"Ah."

"Does that make me a dork?"

"It makes you a wonderful son, and a really sweet man."

"I hope you get to experience that one day," he tells me.

"Experience, what?"

"A wonderful family. A big, loving family. One who never leaves."

I'm silent for a long time, tears escaping down my cheeks. "People always leave, Matthew."

"What do you mean?" he whispers.

"It's what they do. It's built into the fabric of life—if someone doesn't leave you voluntarily, they die. It's just what happens." I think of my parents leaving me in the middle of the night. I think of Eduardo, the only guy I really let myself envision a future with. Gone. Just like every other guy before and after him.

Matthew lets go of my foot, and there's an immediate coldness there—and it's not only because his hand is gone. He gets up from the couch, and for a second I'm afraid he's going to leave. Then he crouches beside me.

"You know, Monica, it doesn't have to be that way."

He talks to me, then, of hope and faith. Of a God who never leaves.

Have I heard some version of this before? Yes.

Have I ever heard it like this? Never.

And even though a part of me wants to scoff and tell him he's crazy, there's an even bigger part of me that is yearning for this to be true. To be true for *me*.

"Come to church with me, Monica," he says at one point.

At this, I do scoff. "No church wants someone like me anywhere near them."

Matthew, who's sitting on the floor now, propped against the coffee table, sits up, staring intently at me. "What do you mean by that?"

I laugh. "You know exactly what I mean."

"I don't," he says genuinely. "That's why I'm asking."

I wave a hand across my body. "Messed up. 'Sinful,'" I say with air quotes.

"What do you think the point of church is?"

"I dunno, make people feel bad about themselves? Or, maybe to make some elite group of people feel good about themselves for following all the rules."

"Jesus said he came to help the sick."

"Oh, so you *do* think I'm sinful?" I say with a twist of my lips and a raised brow.

"We all are, Monica." Even in the dark, his eyes bore into mine and I can see the depth there. This is no joke for him. "And anyone who makes you feel less-than isn't imitating Jesus."

"That hasn't been my church experience."

"I'm sorry." He says it quietly. His serious eyes are watery in their blue depths.

Ugh. I can't believe this guy is making me consider going to church.

"How do you even know where to go? You've never been here before."

"Well, there's this amazing invention, you may not have heard about it before..." he pulls out his phone and taps it, a smirk on his kissable mouth.

"You dork," I say, grabbing his phone. We wrestle over it until we're both laughing and breathless. His face is so close to mine, I'm breathing his air, and all I can think about is what it would be like to kiss him—for him to *want* me to kiss him.

"I go to spin class Sunday mornings. I never miss."

"We did your thing today," he says, his breath warm on my lips. "How about we do my thing tomorrow?"

I nod, not trusting my voice at the moment. Eventually, he pulls away, a painful extraction that makes me shiver.

"Fine, cowboy. I'll go to church with you. But don't expect me to be a saint."

He nods. "Deal."

When the power comes back on an hour later, I climb into bed, exhausted but hopeful for the first time in a long, long time.

Sexy Priest Vibes

I agonize for a long time over what to wear to church with Matthew. At first, I go for very subdued black pants and black knit sweater—but when I look in the mirror, it's like I'm going to a funeral. Then, I put on my warmeSt dress, but even with leggings on, it's a little bootylicious for church. I flip through my entire closEt three times, wondering if I can wear jeans, if I have to wear a hat (that's a thing at church, right?) or if there are any faux pas that I might accidentally choose that would paint a sCarlet letter on my chest. I text Mila: *What do you wear to church?*

Mila: *We've been going to church in Luke's barn. We wear jeans.*

I gRoan and throw my phone on the bed. *Not helpful, Mila.*

I throw on my robe and stick my hEad out of the door. "Matthew?"

He grunTs from the couch, still half-asleep.

"What do I wear to church?"

"Whatever you want," he calls out.

"Okay, I'll go with the fishnets and leather dress then."

He grunts again, and I hear a shuffling from the living room as he says, "Coming."

He shows up at my bedroom door, his hair sticking out in all different directions, his eyelids fighting to stay open. He looks absolutely adorable and I have to put my hands in my robe pockets so I'll keep them to myself. I tell myself that I *will* respect his boundaries, even if it's becoming increasingly difficult to do so.

"What're we working with?" he asks. I usher him to my closet and show him some options.

"This works," he says, pointing at a sweater and jeans. "I feel like Katie Jo would wear something similar."

I nod, frowning at the idea of looking like his little sister. Not exactly what I'm going for, but it'll have to do for our church outing. "Thanks."

We grab a quick muffin and coffee at the corner coffee shop on our way out, and I feel a little bad to not have something more substantial for Matthew. I know that man needs to eat. He looks extra handsome today, with a fresh button-down shirt under his jacket—as if he'd packed it on purpose to go to church—and his hair brushed off his forehead in an adorable attempt to style his slightly out of control hair. And, of course, he's got his cowboy boots and Wranglers. I wonder if he owns any other type of shoe.

It's sunny but cold today, with piles of snow around the edges of buildings and lamp posts. We practically run through the cold, and I wish Matthew would wrap his arm around me. For more reasons than warmth.

The church we attend is only a few blocks from my apartment, and one of the first things I notice is that there are a lot of people our age in attendance. I half-expected us to go to one of the historic churches that dot the city with their elaborate architecture, but this church meets in a movie theater. As we enter the theater, an usher welcomes us and hands us a battery-operated candle. One of the greeters, a petite girl with braids, compliments my sweater, which makes me feel relieved that I chose a solid option—or, rather, that Matthew chose well for me.

I hesitate at the back of the theater, feeling overwhelmed by where to sit. I don't typically go to places where I don't know where I fit in. This is very outside-the-box for me. We went to mass frequently when I was a kid, but I opted out as a teenager. Even when I went, I'd sit in the back. But this church doesn't seem anything like mass...what kind of church meets in a movie theater? If we sit too close, will the priest call us out? Will it be one of those situations like a comedy night where the comedian picks on the people sitting closest to him?

I'm starting to regret coming when Matthew reaches back and grabs my hand, giving it a comforting squeeze. Thankfully, he doesn't lead me to the front, but instead settles us about three-quarters of the way back. He immediately introduces himself to the person sitting beside him, and pulls me into a polite conversation with the millennial-aged hipster.

The service begins with a choir singing Christmas-themed songs—some I'm familiar with, and others I'm not. Everyone is standing, singing along and swaying to the music. The choir director instructs us to turn on our candles as the theater lights dim, and the effect is a beautiful one. When an older woman gets on the mic and sings "Mary Did You Know" accompanied by the piano and a violin, I get lost in the song.

After the singing, we take our seats and a man comes up. He certainly doesn't look like a priest—not with his black jeans and casual button down shirt. Even his boots give him a cool-guy edge. Oh my gosh, maybe he *is* a comedian. I crouch down in my seat a little more, and Matthew gives me a glance. I want to wave him away, not to draw attention to me unnecessarily. I don't want this priest-comedian guy looking at me.

As I start to pay more attention to what he's saying than what he's wearing or where I'm sitting, I realize he's talking about the story of Christmas—that God came down in human form in order to save us from ourselves. When he speaks about how we all have a God-shaped hole in our lives that we try to fill with other things, I feel a ripple of emotion that I desperately try to quell. I don't want to feel anything right now—not at *church*. I'm not trying to come back here. Especially not without Matthew.

And, yet...I listen.

"Some of us try to fill that hole with work, with relationships, with hobbies, or even with drinking or drugs," he says. "I know I did that before I really knew what God was all about. I was going from thing to thing to thing to try to keep myself together, thinking that I could only come to God once I was 'good.' But then I found the most amazing thing—I could fall apart with God. And I did, I let all my walls fall, let myself just be a mess with him. And now, I'm totally fixed." He holds out his hands, as if to say, 'Look at me, I'm awesome.' But then, he waves his hands. "Just kidding, I'm still a mess." Everyone laughs. "But I'm a *loved* mess."

Something about his words make my nose tingle and my eyes prick with tears. And before I can help it, they start to fall unbidden. Because he seemed to express my exact desire: to be a *loved* mess. Prior to today, I wouldn't have thought it was possible, but now...I'm not so sure.

I feel Matthew's eyes on me, but I won't look at him. Not with wet eyes. Still, he reaches over and grabs my hand, tucking it into his. The very act of him holding my hand seems to make the walls that have been cracking finally crumble. The tears fall freely as I confront—perhaps for the first time in my life—how badly I want to be loved, even if I'm a mess.

After the service, we chat with a few people around us and one girl even gets my number and we set up a time to get coffee together this week. I didn't expect church people to be so approachable, but then again maybe I'm just desperate for something *real* for the first time.

Matthew and I head to lunch across the street, and I grill him with questions about church, God, and the Bible.

"That priest guy—"

"The pastor?"

"He's not a priest?"

Matthew shakes his head.

"Wait, so can he get married?"

"Yep." He takes a big bite of his sub and then, with a full mouth, says, "My dad's a pastor, you know."

"Ah, you're one of those, then," I tease, stabbing at my salad.

"What does that mean?"

"You're either a goodie two shoes, or you're a wild one. Not much in between."

He leans back in his chair, a glint in his eye as he stares at me. "And which one am I do you think?" A lock of hair falls in his eye and I want with everything in me to reach out and brush it out of the way.

"Goodie two shoes, obviously," I say, though even as I say it, it feels inaccurate. Sure, Matthew's had boundaries, but he's never made me feel bad about my choices. He didn't condemn me for drinking, or trying to hook up with him. "Am I wrong?"

He chuckles. "My siblings would get a kick out of you saying that."

"So, what? You already sowed your wild oats or something?"

He takes a bite of his sandwich, seeming to consider his response. "You don't become a bull rider without sowing *some* wild oats."

"Sure, your life is a wild oat-fest," I deadpan.

He laughs, shaking his head, and I burst into a giggle.

"Nah, Matthew, you totally give off priest vibes."

This makes him choke on his sandwich. "Priest vibes?" he exclaims.

I glance up, as if I'm considering my words. "Okay, maybe, like, sexy priest vibes."

At this, he reddens, but a smile cracks through the embarrassment. "That ain't a thing."

"I didn't think it was either till I met you."

He snorts, half-choking on his sandwich again. "And you?"

"*Moi*?" I shake my head. "I don't think I give off sexy priest vibes," I say with a wink.

A rare and precious dimple appears in his cheek, and it takes everything in me to not reach over and run my fingertip over it. He levels his gaze at me. "What I mean, Monica, is: what about your life? Is it a 'wild oat fest'?"

I press my lips together, knowing that Matthew saw a glimpse of my oats—very wild and free—the first night he came here. He *knows*. "I think my wild oats need a break." I look down at my salad, toying with the lettuce with my fork. This suddenly feels very vulnerable.

"Like a temporary break, or hanging up your boots kind of break?" I can hear all the questions wrapped up in this one thing he's asking me, and it feels monumental. I take a moment to really think about my response: *what do I really want*? Do I want to keep going down the path I was on, or do I want something else? Something new?

"An indefinite break. Maybe...permanent."

He holds my gaze for a long time, and then says, "I'd like that," as if I'd just told him I'd like to spend forever with him.

And, maybe, in a small way, I just did.

My phone buzzes with a text from Mila, saying they're on their way to the airport. Third time's a charm, I hope. I wonder what Mila will make of this new version of me. And in a way, it doesn't matter—because this is who I am. Mila will love me no matter what. It feels good to recognize that, and a quiet confidence settles in my chest.

As we finish our lunch, Matthew gets a call from a friend. I can tell by the voice on the other line that it's a female, and I've immediately got my defenses up. When he gets off the phone, he says, "That was my friend, Sarah. She's performing at the event with her horse. She does trick riding like Katie Jo does."

"Cool," I say, though I feel anything but cool right now. I know we were just in church, but I hate Sarah, and anyone else named Sarah, and anyone *thinking* about naming their kid Sarah. All because she has Matthew's number, and he had a rare smile on his face when he picked up the phone. I feel possessive over that smile. I only want it to belong to me.

"Anyway, her horse was trailered up here with some friends but she's flying in. Her flight doesn't get in till tomorrow and her buddy who was supposed to take care of her horse has appendicitis and is currently going into surgery."

"Ouch."

"She asked if I could go check on her horse, stretch his legs and feed him, that sort of thing."

I nod, still trying to overcome my feelings toward a woman I've never met.

"Want to come with me?"

I laugh, flipping my hair over my shoulder in an act of nonchalance I don't feel. "I have a policy about things: unless I can do it in heels, I just won't do it."

"Is that so?" Matthew leans forward, a smile playing on his lips. "What about your precious spin class?"

"I can do spin class in heels, I just choose not to."

"Well theoretically you could ride a horse in heels, but today you could choose not to."

"Hard to argue with that point."

"I'm a tough man to argue with, Monica."

"I'm beginning to see that, Matty."

He barks out a laugh as he stands up. "Nobody calls me Matty," he says.

I stand beside him, a little closer than absolutely necessary, and look up at him. "Well, it's a good thing I'm not nobody."

This gets a small smile, almost bashful, from him, and I have to bite my lip to keep from breaking out in my own wide grin. Sarah didn't get *that* smile. Matthew grabs my hat from the table and tucks it on my head in a surprisingly intimate gesture. "That's true," he says, and I can't even hold back my smile.

An hour later, we're driving in an Uber to a farm in New Jersey. I'm still trying to wrap my mind around the bull riding event tomorrow as I question Matthew about the details.

"So you're telling me that tomorrow night there will be a whole bunch of bulls and horses and other animals inside Madison Square Garden?" I knew the bull riding event was in New York, I just didn't realize it was in the heart of the city. Matthew nods. "I don't get it, where do they keep all the bulls for this event?"

"It's kind of like with the horses, they keep them at different barns near the area. Sarah's horse for example is just one of I think five others that came up for this event with hers."

"Snap. I never knew."

"You gonna come watch me?" He glances at me out of the corner of his eye, as if he's afraid to really look at me. Is he afraid I'll say no? His hand, which is resting on the middle console next to mine—close, but not touching—twitches closer to mine.

"I'd like that," he says, repeating his earlier phrase and this time I'm sure it's equally loaded with meaning.

"I'll be there, then."

He smiles, ducking his head to hide it. My heart squeezes at this massive cowboy who's reticent and sweet. Where do they even make guys like this? If you'd told me about him last week, I wouldn't have believed you. And yet, here I am.

I glance out the window, and that's when I feel his pinky finger graze mine. I inch my hand nearer to his until the tips of my fingers are underneath his. Electricity is zinging across my fingers, up my arm and straight into my chest, where it pings around wildly. I glance over at Matthew, wondering if he's feeling the same things I am.

He flicks his eyes at our hands, and then back to my eyes, as if to ask, *Is this okay?* I laugh quietly, taking his hand fully in mine, twining our fingers together.

And let me tell you, holding someone's hand has never felt so good.

Though I'm not really a horse person, I have to admit that when our Uber driver rolls down the driveway of the farm, it's like a breath of fresh air. Especially after the press and chaos of the city, being in an open space is very freeing.

The barn itself smells like farm animals, but also something else that's appealing—like fresh cut wood. It's warm and earthy, and I feel grounded just by being here.

Sarah's horse, a light brown boy ("a chestnut gelding" Matthew tells me) named Hercules, makes a low rumbling sound when he sees Matthew. We stopped for apples on our way here, and Matthew procures one for the horse, who sticks out his lip to test the fruit. Once he approves, he bites into it, cutting the apple in half. "Want to feed him the other half?" Matthew asks. I shake my head no, but Matthew beckons me over, taking my hand. I sigh. I'm getting way too used to Matthew holding my hand, and it's going to be painful when he's gone. He pulls my glove off, then props up my hand with his, plopping the apple into the center of my palm. "Keep it flat," he tells me, and then presses my hand under the horse's nose. It's an odd sensation, as the horse gobbles the apple using his whiskered mouth. I can't help but giggle at the feeling.

Matthew walks into the horse's stall, putting his halter on, explaining to me what he's doing as he goes. Once the horse is haltered, he beckons me into the stall. This time, I shake my head more forcefully. "Nah, I'm gonna pass."

"C'mon, Monica. Trust me."

I sigh and step over the lip of the stall, my heeled boots crunching into the wood shavings. Once I'm close enough, Matthew wraps an arm around my back, pulling me until I'm in front of him, with the horse right in front of me. Hercules is so close he could stomp on my feet if he wanted to.

"The first thing you need to know about horses," Matthew says as he takes my hand, pressing it flat against Hercules' shoulder, "is that they don't *want* to hurt you. At their core, they are gentle herd animals whose primary desire is just like ours: to be loved."

The warmth of Hercules's skin permeates my skin, and I soak it in. Hercules takes a deep breath, and inadvertently, I do the same. In this moment, I feel a peace I've rarely, if ever, experienced. I'm enveloped by two very sturdy beings—Matthew, his solid chest against my back, his hand steadying mine, and Hercules, the muscular yet calm horse beneath my hand. The horse turns his head back to look at us, nuzzling at Matthew, and then me. I laugh as Hercules's nose tickles my side, Matthew holding me in place with his arm.

And for the first time in a long time, I am happy.

Oh Mi-ami

I would prefer to just watch Matthew clean this horse and exercise him—but of course Matthew involves me in everything. Except for cleaning the horse's feet—I draw the line there. But that doesn't mean I can't enjoy watching Matthew pick his feet.

Once the horse is saddled, we walk to an indoor arena via a covered walkway. Other horses in their stalls put their heads over the doors, whickering at us. At the arena, I lean my elbows on the wall and watch as Matthew smoothly lifts himself onto the horse's back and begins to walk him around. He's in a different type of saddle than I'm used to seeing Mila in—Matthew called it a western saddle. It has a big horn that seems like it would be painful if your nether regions collided with it. Other than that, it does seem safer than Mila's barely-there saddle.

Although safety doesn't really seem to be in Matthew's wheelhouse. Unlike every time I've seen Mila ride, he's not wearing a helmet, though he did bring one out and placed it on the edge of the ring.

Matthew trots the horse around, and I'm struck by how effortless their movements are. It's as if the horse and Matthew are conjoined, the two of them no longer individual beings. I search for the tiny movements that would indicate Matthew's telling the horse what to do, but I can't discern anything. It's kind of amazing.

When he's done, Matthew asks, "Want a turn?"

I laugh, shaking my head yet again, but that hasn't gotten me very far with this trip to the barn, has it?

I walk out into the arena, my legs trembling a bit at the thought of getting on this massive animal. He gives me a short safety briefing, fits the helmet on me, and helps me onto the horse using a mounting block. He shows me how to hold the reins, adjusting them in my hands.

"You sure Sarah would be okay with this?" I ask, trying to ascertain how important this Sarah chick is.

"I asked her, she's cool with it. Besides, I know Hercules well. Sarah boards him at my parents' barn." The jealousy I feel at Sarah's proximity to Matthew's family home burns like acid down my throat. I audibly sigh in relief when Matthew says, "She's a family friend," emphasizing *friend*.

At first, Matthew walks beside Hercules and me, giving me instructions about how to steer. One thing is for sure: I'm a lot less smooth than Matthew. He made this look easy, whereas I'm sure I look like a clod.

Eventually, Matthew starts giving me little challenges: turn here, make a circle, change directions. He starts jogging around backward, zigzagging around the arena while I attempt to steer Hercules to follow him. Hercules makes it easy—he wants to follow Matthew seemingly as much as I do. After a while, all of my fears fall away and I'm just lost in the moment.

"I could do that again," I tell Matthew once I pull up Hercules at the end of my ride.

"Yeah?"

Matthew helps me dismount, and suddenly I'm flush with him, his chest against mine, our eyes locking. "Yeah," I say weakly, though my thoughts are skittering all over the place. *I could definitely do* this *again.*

And then, Matthew's eyes flick—undeniably—to my mouth, then back up again to my eyes. *Oh Mi-ami.* Matthew Craig wants to kiss me. I know it as well as I know the Kate Spade catalog. Which is to say, *I know.* The moment stretches for a long time, with neither one of us making a move. I remind myself that I will respect Matthew's boundaries, his convictions. I will not be the one to make the first move here.

But, oh I want to.

Matthew reaches up and unclips my helmet, tugging it off of my head. And I think, *this is it.* He's going to kiss me.

"I'm glad you had fun," he says, his voice low and a little husky.

"I had a great time, the whole day," I say honestly, surprised by my admission that I had a good time at church. Elizabeth wouldn't believe me if I told her.

"I'm glad," Matthew says with a nod, then he pulls away from me. It feels like someone just ripped wax off my brow before I was ready when Matthew turns to lead Hercules out of the arena. Without kissing me.

Back in Manhattan, the sun is setting as we order food to the apartment and sit around in our sweats as we wait for Mila and Alex to get in.

"So, what's your cowboy getup look like?" I ask with a waggle of my eyebrows, hoping to see him blush.

Pink crests his cheekbones, spreading to the tips of his ears.

Mission accomplished.

"Whatd'ya mean?"

"Do you have those leather legging things with the fringes?"

"You mean chaps? Yeah, I've got a pair. It doesn't have fringes though."

I pretend to pout. "That's a shame. I like the fringes. They're spicy."

This gets a laugh out of him, and it's so big and loud I want to pump my fist in the air. Ten points for Gryffindor.

And to anyone who argues that I don't belong in Gryffindor, I say this: that's the house I choose.

We've fallen into an easy camaraderie with each other, with a ribbon of tension flowing between us every time we touch. We're back on the couch, Matthew on one side, me on the other, our feet meeting in the middle under a blanket. And, let it be known, feet have never felt so good. I can't even believe I'm saying that, but I'm a changed woman. I mean, look at me: going to church, riding a horse, enjoying the simple—almost chaste—touches of this man.

I'm finding that there's something deliciously sweet in holding back. In the past, by putting all my cards out on the table—and, somehow, simultaneously, revealing *nothing* real—I've missed this. This thrill of restraint, of the almost-touch, the mere brush of skin rather than plunging headfirst into oblivion. It's like I'm fully alive for the first time.

And, I think, I'm having a similar effect on Matthew. The barely-smiling man who showed up on my doorstep a few days ago is finally loosening up into a sunny version of himself. And I adore it.

I have this thought pop into my head unbidden: I could do this forever. I could make it my life's goal to make this man laugh, to live to see his smile.

I just wonder if he'll let me.

Nails of Death

Mila and Alex finally arrive, looking worn down after battling through two of the busiest airports during the holidays. I had offered to pay for their Uber from JFK *before* I lost my job, but I haven't even told Mila about it yet, so I take the hit to my bank account. I'm just glad to finally have my best friend in town. I'm almost relieved for a reprieve from the tension between Matthew and me. If this guy doesn't kiss me soon, I might spontaneously combust.

After big hugs and lots of squealing, I get the newlyweds settled in my bedroom—I'm crashing in Elizabeth's room while she's in Connecticut for the holidays with her family—and then we reconvene in the living room. Alex shows us a game called *Brilliant or BS* that one of their staff introduced to them. It's similar to *Balderdash*, except instead of coming up with phony definitions, there's a multiple choice question and each player has to convince the judge that they know the answer—even if they don't. The judge then has to guess who's brilliant and who's totally faking it.

An hour in, Alex and I are tied for being brilliant—Alex beCause he's actually brilliant, and me because I'm apparently really good at faking it. I'd be more sad about this if I weren't winning. Of course, I'm up against sOme of the most genuine people in this world, so it's not exactly steep competition. Poor Matthew can't lie to save his life, but that's fine by me.

We deciDe we all need hot chocolate, so Matthew and I are in the kitchen heating up the milk when he asks me if I have any wrapping paper for the gifts he bought for his mom and sister. I grab a tubE from under my bed and tell him, "You never told me the worst gift you ever got from your brothers."

He shakes his head. "I ain't telling."

"Matthew! After everything we've been through." I sidle closer to him and give him my best puppy dog eyes, but he's an expert at avoiding eye contact, so it's useless. He continues on, pouring cocoa powder into the milk as if the conversation is done.

He clearly doesn't know me that well if he thinks I'm going to drop this.

"Matthew…" I grab his arm, poking him in the side until he tells me. He starts laughing hysterically—I clearly found his ticklish spot. "Stop! Stop!" he cries, squirming away from me and spilling milk all over the counters. I don't care, I'm not letting up until he tells me.

Also, this giant of a man writhing around from a little tickle is too much for me. Can't stop, won't stop, you know what I'm saying?

Finally, Matthew gains enough control over himself to grab my hands. He holds up my fingers, staring at my red nails and says, "What are these? Nails of death?"

"The better to tickle you with, my dear," I say with a cackling witch's voice. I extract my hand from his and lunge to tickle him again, which only makes him shriek with laughter. And, of course, I can't let up now that I've found my secret weapon to make Matthew laugh. His laugh is infectious—I'm pretty sure it's the best sound I've ever heard in my entire life.

Eventually Matthew tugs me against his chest, pinning my arms to my side as he wraps his arms around me. We're both breathing hard, still laughing.

"I found your weakness," I tell him breathlessly.

"I'll give you my life's savings to keep you from telling my brothers."

"I'll never give up my leverage. Besides, I think your life savings could buy, like, half of my Chelsea boots."

"That may be true, but imagine the price of my loyalty if you keep my secret."

"Hmm."

I don't even remember what we're discussing because all I can think of is how good it feels to be in Matthew's arms. To feel his chest against mine, his heart hammering away. His breath is coming in short puffs that I feel against my cheek. If I just stood on tiptoe…

"You guys need some help?" Mila's voice cuts through the moment, and Matthew and I practically jump away from each other.

"All good in the hood," I say, and Mila raises both eyebrows at me. I don't have to look over at Matthew to know he's blushing furiously, and the thought only makes my heart race even more.

"I'll, uh, get a towel for this mess," Matthew mumbles, bypassing two kitchen towels as he flees.

"Guess we have some catching up to do," Mila says under her breath. I simply smile and shrug, as if everything is right in the world.

And, maybe—just maybe—it is.

The Convert

The next morning, I wake up early and head to the corner market where I grab eggs, bacon, and biscuits—the break-and-bake kind. I make breakfast for Matthew since he has to leave early to get to his event. He's sitting on the barstools of our kitchen island—we don't have enough room for a proper table, so this is where we eat if not on the couch—in his full cowboy getup, including the hat. A week ago, I would've said cowboys were lame. But now...dunk me in water and consider me a convert, because I am *all* about this.

"I asked to work the set up crew, for the extra cash, but also," he glances up at me with an apologetic grin, "I didn't know how it would go here. If I'd want an excuse to leave."

I scoop some scrambled eggs onto his plate. "And how do you feel now?" I ask him with all the feigned confidence in the world—though my heart is tumbling through my chest as I wait for his response.

"Now I wish..." he cuts himself off, shaking his head. I wait for him to finish, but he never does because Alex comes in, searching for coffee for Mila. Before we can return to our conversation, Matthew's gobbled his food and donned his backpack. "I'll see you there?" he asks as Alex darts back into the room with coffee.

I nod, every part of me wanting to hook a finger through his jeans and tug him close to me. But I refrain. I'm afraid he's going to leave with simply a nod, or one of those cowboy hat touches, but right before he turns on his heel, he leans in and presses his lips against my cheek.

Ten minutes after Matthew's gone, my cheek is still burning with the feel of his lips. I seriously may never wash my face again, because I never want this feeling to go away. Who knew a kiss to the cheek could feel so...precious?

Mila finally stumbles from my bedroom, looking sleep rumbled and an overall hot mess. She glances around the kitchen at the remnants of the breakfast I cooked for Matthew.

"Your sad excuse for cooking may cut it for Matthew, but it's not why we came to New York," she teases.

"And here I thought you came to see me," I say, whipping a kitchen towel at her bottom.

"Monica, I thought you of all people would know why Mila goes anywhere," Alex says.

"For the sweets. I know, I know."

"You're a very close second, though," Mila says, enveloping me in a hug. "Now that Matthew's gone, I'm going to need an update, stat." Mila waggles her brows at me.

I groan, pulling away from Mila. "Nothing is going on." Nothing except a kiss on the cheek—which, for old Monica would be about as exciting as a fist bump. But, with Matthew, it feels like the beginning of something.

Alex and Mila exchange a knowing glance. "Doesn't look like nothing," Alex says.

Mila gestures at the pans in the sink. "I lived with you for how many years? Three?" She dips her fingers into the soapy water covering the pans. "I never once got breakfast," she says as she flicks soap bubbles at me.

"Hey! Don't start what you can't finish, Mila Caballero," I say as I grab the sink nozzle and point it at her.

"Surrender! White flag!" she screeches before I can turn on the water.

"Smart chica." I put the nozzle back. "Want to go get pastries?"

Mila sighs dramatically. "I thought you'd never ask."

We're heading to Maman—a French bakery and one of my favorite cafés—when I get a text from an old figure skating friend, Gloria: *Did you see this?* She texts me a screenshot of a pregnancy announcement. A beautiful woman with cascading blonde curls, a slightly protruding belly, and a man's hands wrapped possessively around her waist. It takes me a moment to realize who the man is.

Eduardo.

The singular man I let past my walls—if only partially—in all my years of dating. The only guy I ever said I love you to. With him, I felt infinite. I even had a Pinterest board—secret, of course—filled with wedding inspiration. *That* got deleted when he broke up with me and immediately started dating this wholesome blondie named Mary. I mean who names their kid Mary in this century? Come *on*.

When Eduardo broke up with me and got together with his now-wife, he said, "She's the kind of woman you start a family with." Implying, of course, that I was deficient in that way.

And maybe I was. Maybe I still am. But it doesn't stop me from wanting that—from *hoping* that someone would see past my walls enough to fight for me. To fight for the real me.

I wanted that with Eduardo, but it has to be a two-way street. And I just wasn't his cup of tea, Mary is. They were engaged a mere six months after our breakup, married a year later. And of course they'll have perfect Instagram-worthy children with mochaccino skin and green eyes, defying every law of genetics.

I shove my phone into the back pocket of my jeans, trying not to cry. Honestly, it's not about Eduardo anymore. I couldn't care less about that guy.

I'm beginning to realize that Eduardo was just filling a void that my parents had left in my life—and I think, in a way, I was filling a void for him, too. A final indulgence before he was ready to get serious with his life. And of course that led me to believe I wasn't 'serious' material for anyone—when in reality, I was just too young for Eduardo. But the way it all went down, I felt like I had to put up walls and shield myself from anyone who might reject me.

Being with Matthew these past few days, it's the first time in years I've wanted something *more* with a guy. With anyone, if I'm being honest. And that terrifies me.

Because I'm ready to let my walls down, to let Matthew see the real me. I've already started to do that with him, and he's not running away screaming, so I suppose that's a good sign. But I'm scared that behind those walls, there's nothing substantial. That all this time, what I've been guarding is meaningless.

As we ride the subway to Maman, I take out my phone and look at the picture Matthew took of me in Times Square for the first time. I almost gasp, because I don't look like me at all. There's something in my eyes that's just a little bit broken, but also...a little bit beautiful. I stare at the picture for a while before tucking my phone away. I can be *that* Monica. I think.

Seeing Eduardo and his wife *pregnant*, and realizing how much power I've let his rejection have over me, I decide it's time. Time to let go. Time to let the walls fall. Not with everyone all at once, but with the people who really matter. I'll let them see the real me.

Starting with Mila.

When we walk into the café and settle at a table, I turn to her and grab her hand. "I got fired from my job."

"Oh, Mon." Mila pulls me into a hug and then, saint that she is, looks up at Alex and says, "Can you get us coffee?" He gives a two-finger salute and Mila adds, "And every chocolate pastry on the menu!"

"Wouldn't dream of doing otherwise," he says with a soft smile, and then leans down to give her a lingering kiss.

Ugh. These two and their perfection, it makes me nauseous.

Nauseous, and also slightly jealous.

I want this. And not just with anyone. With *Matthew*.

Once Alex walks away, Mila turns back to me, grabbing my hand in both of hers. "I'm so sorry, Mon. Tell me everything."

I tell her about what it was like working at Goldman Sachs, how I morphed myself into a subgenre of Monica in order to fit into the bro culture. How I had to take a stand against the Ashton's of the world, but took it too far. To the point of getting fired for my demeaning and crass remarks. It doesn't matter that Ashton said the same things—if not worse. I'm responsible for my own self, not anyone else.

"I need to find a job," I tell her. "But the thing is, I don't think I want to keep working in places like Goldman. That's just not the kind of person I want to be anymore. I don't even know where to start if I'm going to branch out from that, though."

We talk for a few minutes about what I could do instead of being an analyst and then Mila leans forward and says, "What I really want to know is what's going on with Matthew. Like, for real."

At this point, Alex sits down with all of our coffees and pastries and says, "Yes, girl, sip the tea," in a voice that sounds like he's trying to mock me. "Or is it spill the tea? I'm not really sure. Are we sipping or spilling?" He shakes his head, like he can't be bothered to keep up with Gen Z trends.

"Right now, we're just drinking coffee, Alex," I tell him as I take a sip of my mocha with an exaggerated eye roll. Before I complete the sip, Mila snatches it from my hand.

"No coffee for you until you spill the tea about Matthew."

"Hey! No fair!" But Mila's already handed my coffee back to Alex, who's guarding it seriously. "Fine," I groan. "But I'm warning you, there's not much to tell."

I tell them, haltingly, about my foolish attempt at using Matthew as my weekend distraction, and then finally giving up—and giving in—to his contagious goodness. I tell them about starting to let my walls down, about our late-night conversation about my parents leaving me in Colombia and what that did for my anxiety about relationships. I even tell them about finding out that Eduardo's wife is pregnant, and how that brings up all of my fears and insecurities. Of course Alex doesn't know about Eduardo, but Mila was my roommate my freshman year when we broke up and remembers the fall out. "I've allowed my fear of being abandoned to control me, to force people away. I'd rather be in control of leaving than show someone my real self, and for *them* to choose to leave *me*. But Matthew's making me rethink all of that." I'm about to tell them about going to church, when I feel a hand on my shoulder.

"Monica?"

I turn in my seat to find Helen. My boss from Goldman Sachs. She's holding about a zillion shopping bags—clearly doing some last minute Christmas shopping—and there's a soft smile on her face. "Hey, Helen," I say, introducing her briefly to Mila and Alex.

"Sorry to interrupt your time with your friends, but I couldn't help but overhear you talking while I was waiting in line..." When I hear this, a full-on blush creeps up my face. Matthew must be rubbing off on me, and I'm slightly mortified that Helen heard all of that. "And, I just wanted to say, Monica, I'm amazed by how you've changed in just a few short days. You don't even sound like the Monica I know," she says with a laugh that I should find offensive, but I don't. I *have* changed. Like, *a lot*. "Anyway, whatever your next move is, count me as an ally. I'll write you a recommendation or call potential employers, whatever you need, I'm your girl."

"Wow, thanks, Helen." I stand up and give her a hug, and then a kiss on the cheek, Spanish-style.

"I'm proud of you," she says. "And, for what it's worth, it sounds like Matthew is a catch. Don't let your fear of rejection stop you from putting your heart out there. At the very least you'll learn from it, and at the most you'll have a forever kind of love." She says this wistfully, and I wonder what she's experienced to say this to me. But I trust her.

Her phone starts ringing and she startles. "Oh! I've got to get that. Don't be a stranger, Mon. Have a happy Christmas!" She nods her goodbyes to Alex and Mila and hustles out of the shop and onto the street to answer her phone.

I slump back in my chair. "That was...unexpected."

"That was incredible. I'd give my right pinkie finger to hear my boss say that to me," Mila says.

"Mila, *you* are your boss," Alex says.

"I know, but like, if I had a boss."

"I could say those things to you," he says with a raise of his brow.

Mila leans in to her husband's chest and whispers, "I have some other things I think I'd like for you to say..."

"Oooookay, children," I say, standing up. "Whatd'ya want to do next? I'm game for whatever as long as it's PG-13." I give them a scolding look because they're staring at each other in a way that is not at all PG-13.

"I thought you had like a whole weekend planned for us?" Mila says.

"Uh, yeah, that was two days ago! I did all the stuff I had planned with Matthew."

"Laaaame."

"Zero regrets."

Mila laughs, "How about you finish your coffee and then we can make a plan?" Mila hands me back my coffee. "And you get a pastry for good behavior."

"Just one?" I say, eyeing the massive box of pastries Alex picked out.

"Don't be greedy, girl."

I grab two pastries—a chocolate croissant and some kind of cinnamon roll that looks magical—and Mila shakes her head at me. We savor our pastries and coffee, sipping out of the classic blue and white floral cups.

When we walk out of the pastry shop, Mila loops her arm through mine. "I'm happy for you, Mon."

"Don't be just yet," I say with a sigh. "He's not quite mine."

"Not yet," Mila says with a squeeze of my arm.

"I feel like this is the start of a rom-com where the best friend comes in town and tries to help the heroine win over the guy of her dreams," Alex says. "There should be a Taylor Swift song playing right now." He starts humming "Welcome to New York" under his breath. I laugh, enjoying this carefree Alex that I've never seen before—he's always been so serious and, honestly, kind of burdened. But marrying Mila and getting residency in the States, it's like it's lifted a thousand pound weight off of him.

"You been watching a lot of rom-coms, Alex?" I tease.

Alex shrugs, completely secure in his manhood. "He likes them," Mila says.

"Uh, correction: I like you. The rom-coms are incidental."

Mila leans in closer to me and mock-whispers, "He *really* likes the rom-coms. He'll watch them without me."

"Babe!"

"What? It's true. Own it."

Alex shrugs again. "Whatever. What're we doing? Mission: win over Matthew?"

Mila takes Alex's hand. "I don't think Monica needs any help with that, my love. Why don't we go sightseeing instead?"

Cowpeople

We do all the typical New York touristy things until it's time to get ready to head to the event tonight. I don't spend very long agonizing over what to wear—I just put on whatever feels good to me. It's not trendy, it's not necessarily comfortable, but it feels like *me.*

"We'll have to be extra loud tonight," Mila says when we're on the subway. "It looks like Mr. and Mrs. Craig, Anya, Luke, and John aren't going to make it in time. Their flight got delayed until late tonight. Hopefully he moves on to the next round so they can see him on Wednesday."

"Katie Jo and Mikey made it on though, right?" Alex asks. I don't know how anyone can keep track of this massive family, but Mila and Alex are doing their darnedest.

I'm obviously sad for Matthew that hIs whole family won't be here to see him, but I'm also a little relieved that I won't have to meet his parents right now. I'm not sure I'm readY for that yet.

Madison Square Garden is humming with activity and *a lot* of cowboys. And cowgirls. Cow*people*? Is that a thing? Who knew so many people in New YorK liked this sort of thing?

The vibes around the arena are carnival-like. There's face painting, balloon animals, and some sort of game that involves throwing ropes at a bar—on second thought, maybe that's not a game and it's just a bunch of drunk guYs throwing ropes? Who knows.

Apparently, Matthew's family is 'Rodeo Royalty'—I don't know what that means, but Alex said it in a way that it has to be taKen seriously. They have a special VIP table that's front and center near the arena floor. Matthew's sister, Katie Jo, waves us down. She's a super cute blondie with hot pink tips and she's every inch a cowgirl—she could totally be in an ad for cowgirl boots or something. When she meets me, she gives me a huge hug.

"Oh my gosh, girl," she says in an intense twang that makes me smile, "Matthew's been sending us all those pictures y'all have been taking. I love it! How did you get him to go on top of the Rock?" She's practically screeching with delight, and her enthusiasm is infectious.

"He seemed nervous, but he didn't fight me much on it."

"That's a miracle straight from baby Jesus himself," she says with a laugh.

"I didn't realize baby Jesus did miracles," her brother, Mikey, says with a teasing poke.

"He's Jesus, he can do miracles whenever he wants to, *Michael*," Katie Jo says with an eye roll.

"We actually have a tradition in Colombia that involves baby Jesus," I say, happy to have something relatively religious to share in this group.

"Oh really?" Mila asks, surprised. I *never* talk about Colombia. Or Jesus for that matter.

I nod. "You know, we celebrate Christmas on Christmas Eve, we call it *Noche Buena*. 'Good Night.' We usually do a lot of dancing, eating, singing, that sort of thing. But at midnight we open presents, instead of on Christmas morning like you guys. My aunt would always say they were from *niño* Jesus. I didn't even know about Santa until I came to the States."

"Oh my gosh I love that!" Katie Jo says.

"I didn't know that," Mila says.

"Maybe we should do a Noche Buena celebration tonight," Alex says. "I mean, maybe we won't do any gifts, but we could figure out something else to do."

Katie Jo and Mila are quick to voice their agreement. "Let's think of what we can do," Katie Jo says.

"Definitely eat," Mila quips.

"*Always* with the eating," I say with a smile.

"Speaking of," Mila says. "I'm going to get a pretzel and a Coke. Anyone want anything?" I decide to go with her, and we take drink and snack orders.

While we're waiting in line, Mila says, "I'm glad you told us about the Noche Buena thing." She loops her arm through mine. "I never hear you talk about Colombia. I should ask about it more."

I shrug. "I should bring it up more. It's not all bad memories, but I think my time there is tainted in my memory."

Mila nods. "That makes a lot of sense. I don't really remember anything from when we lived in Ukraine, but I'm glad we have our traditions. Those are important, it's part of who we are, you know?"

I give her a slight smile. "Marriage has changed you for the better, chica." I put my arm around her and squeeze. I'm tucked under her arm, and she leans down her head to rest on mine. That's when I realize I have a type: all of my friends are so much taller than me. Maybe I need shorter friends.

"I hope you'll get this one day soon," she says.

"Me too." The words—and the hope with which they're said—almost choke my voice, but I manage to get them out. Hope is dangerous—but it's beautiful.

When we get back to the table, Katie Jo attaches herself to me in an endearing way. As standoffish as Matthew was when we first met, Katie Jo is the opposite. She's a big feeler, clearly—she's so expressive, and is constantly grabbing my arm or slapping my shoulder when she says something. It's hilarious and also really cute.

Finally, the lights dim and an announcer's voice booms over the speakers. A shiver of excitement goes through me and then seems to ripple through the whole crowd. Beside me, Katie Jo whoops and howls.

I've never experienced anything like this rodeo event. The floor of Madison Square Garden is filled with dirt—or maybe it's clay, it has an almost orange hue to it—and the back of the arena has pens and cattle shoots where the bulls are. The animals make low, deep bellowing sounds that resonate across the arena. The event starts out a little like a sports game, with the national anthem sung by a woman channeling her best Dolly Parton. Then, a pair of horses and riders comes out and they do a trick riding routine. "Hey! That's Hercules!" I shout. "Mila, I rode that horse!"

In all the excitement, I'd forgotten to tell Mila about going to the barn with Matthew. Mila stares at me in disbelief, then starts laughing. "So I try to get you on a horse for, what? Five years? Then a cute guy shows up and it takes him two days?" She shakes her head, but she's smiling.

Eventually, the announcer calls out the bull riders for the night, one by one onto a platform in the center of the arena. When they introduce Matthew, our table hoots and hollers until I'm sure we'll all lose our voices. He glances our way, giving a small wave and an even smaller smile. Seeing him makes my stomach flip in a way that scared me only twenty-four hours ago—but now it excites me.

I'm totally falling for this guy.

And I'm letting myself do it now, too.

Someone comes out and prays over the bull riders, which only serves to ramp up my nerves. I mean, what kind of sport requires prayer before starting? Yeesh.

Then, the bull riding starts. And I am not even a little prepared for how dangerous this sport is. These bulls are insanely massive, and they're bucking like their lives depend on it. How anyone can hang on for any length of time is impressive, but when Katie Jo tells me that the goal is to hang on for at least eight seconds, I'm surprised. What kind of sport lasts for eight seconds?

I'll tell you one thing: a man came up with this sport. You get a million women in a room and not once, ever, will they come up with something as nuts as bull riding. And whose idea was it that they have to hold on with *one hand*?

So when Katie Jo gestures to the cattle shoot and I see Matthew straddling the fence, getting ready for his ride, I feel like I'm going to throw up.

I finally found a guy I want to entrust my heart to, and he's literally trying to kill himself.

I stand up, gripping the arena barrier in front of me. My heart is booming in my chest and sweat has broken out in tiny pinpricks all over my body.

I'm terrified.

Katie Jo seems to sense what I'm feeling, and she comes to stand up next to me, putting an arm around me. "He'll be okay," she says. "He always is."

When Matthew gets on the bull and they open the shoot, a strangled cry escapes from my mouth. The bull is a blur of movement as he kicks his hind legs up, twisting, and turning to get Matthew off his back. I bury my head into Katie Jo, peeking with one eye as Matthew miraculously holds on for what seems like an eternity. He must've won the round by now—for crying out loud someone get him off that thing!

"This is the worst bull of them all!" I say to Katie Jo, because seriously this bull is the worst we've seen all night. He's demon-possessed for sure.

"That'll get him a better score," Katie Jo says, but I don't care about Matthew's score. I just want him alive. And preferably not brain damaged.

Then, Matthew slips just a fraction, losing his grip on the rope around the bull. It seems like he's going to flip under the bull's belly, but at the last moment he catapults himself away from the bull, landing on the ground in a heap. I scream and grip Katie Jo, shaking her in my anxiety. But Matthew rolls away from the bull, as if he's well aware of where the crazy animal is, and stands up.

The rodeo clowns manage to get the bull back to the cattle shoot, and Matthew waves as the crowd cheers, then he disappears to the back too.

I flop into my chair, the adrenaline coming off of me in waves as I lay my head on the table. I'm exhausted, as if I'd just run a marathon instead of watched an eight second bull ride.

How do people do this?

Better yet, how does Matthew's mom watch this happen? *Voluntarily*?

My emotions are all over the place when I turn to Katie Jo, grabbing her arm. "Will you take me to him?" I plead.

"Sure thing, sugar."

I follow Katie Jo almost blindly, weaving around people whose faces are just a blur because all I can think about is Matthew. Matthew with his shy smile. Matthew blushing. Matthew with his gorgeous blue eyes that seem to see right through to my very soul.

He gets me, and I get him—even though we're so wildly different. And for that reason alone, I will not do the very thing I'm *dying* to do right now. The OG Monica would run up to cowboy Matthew, jump in his arms, wrap my legs around him and kiss the living daylights out of that man.

But I won't do it, because I know that's not what Matthew would want me to do. I'll wait for Matthew to kiss me—if he ever wants to, if he ever chooses to.

Oh God, please let him choose me.

It makes no sense—we're even worse than polar opposites, and yet here I am, totally falling for this guy.

No, seeing him on that bull, so close to danger, I can say confidently I've fallen. I'm a goner.

Oh, God.

We come to the end of a hallway, with security blocking the way. Katie Jo flashes an ID badge of some sort, and he lets her through, but holds out a hand to stop me.

"She's not a buckle chaser, Bill," Katie Jo says in her tart Southern voice. I don't know what a buckle chaser is, but if Matthew's wearing the buckle...I shake my head. "She's with me."

The security guard lets me through and Katie Jo grabs my hand. The scent of livestock hits me full force—the earthy smell of clay and cattle. That's when I see him. He's got one boot up on the railing of a cattle shoot, his arm dangling over the bar. His cowboy hat is resting low on his head, blocking my view of his eyes, until he turns and his eyes find mine.

For a moment, we're the only two people in the world. And all of the fears and doubts I'd ever had drop away as I see the rest of my life in this man's eyes.

I don't know how I can feel so sure about Matthew so quickly—it must be a Christmas miracle.

Matthew greets his sister with a hug and a kiss on her cheek, then Katie Jo finds someone else to talk to, leaving us to ourselves. Matthew takes a step closer to me, but not close enough. "Fancy meetin' you here," he says.

I nod, my fingertips itching to reach out and touch him, to put my hands on his chest or run my fingers through the back of his hair. By some small miracle—probably performed by baby Jesus himself—I manage to keep my hands to myself.

Doesn't mean I'm happy about it, though.

"That was amazing," I say, gesturing toward the arena. "I've never seen anything like it."

When Matthew smiles at this, I think he must be the eighth wonder of the world, he's so beautiful.

Finally, *finally,* he steps closer to me, taking my hand and pulling me into a hug. And it's like coming home. "I'm glad you came."

My head rests against his solid chest, hearing the thrumming of his steady heart. "I'm glad you're still alive," I say, tilting my head up to look him in the eye.

He chuckles, his lips parting and then closing again, as if he wants to say more and then doesn't.

Someone calls Matthew's name, and he breaks away from me. I'm happy to find he looks as reluctant as I feel. "I'll find you after," he tells me.

Back at the table, there's only a few more riders left. I barely watch them as I wait for Matthew to reappear. At long last, the final bull rider gets thrown, and they announce the top scores for the night. We holler like we're on fire when Matthew's name is third on the roll call—he'll be moving on to the next round on Wednesday.

"We need to celebrate, y'all," Katie Jo says when Matthew makes it to the table.

"What're we celebratin'?" Matthew asks.

"You still being alive after that-that—whatever you call that," I say.

"Stupidity?" Katie Jo says.

"Idiocy?" Mila chimes in.

"Epic display of manliness?" Mikey says as he fist bumps Matthew.

"Katie Jo don't you start on me, you ride around upside down *and* without a helmet," Matthew says.

"I'll wear one when you wear one."

Matthew crosses his arms. "Maybe I will."

"And maybe you won't," Katie Jo says with an eye roll. "But what we're celebratin' is baby Jesus."

"And you being alive," I add, still grateful for that small miracle.

"You bein' alive on account of baby Jesus."

"Amen," says Mikey.

"What're we doing to celebrate?"

Everyone looks at me, and a slow smile spreads across my face. "I have an idea," I say. "But it'll take some coordination, and some guts."

"He's got the coordination," Mikey says, pointing at Alex. "And I got the guts."

"Pretty sure *I* got the guts," Matthew says, smacking Mikey's head.

"Yeah, my vote's for Matthew having the guts," Mila says. "At least for tonight." She gives a glance at Alex, who mock-whispers, "I wanted the guts tonight. Why do I always have to be the coordination guy?"

"Alright y'all," Katie Jo says, shaking her head as she tries to refocus us all. "Monica, tell us the plan."

I smile, waggling my brows at them. "You guys are *not* ready."

Security, Security

Twenty minutes later, Katie Jo and Mila are distracting the Madison Square Garden security guards while Mikey and Alex play lookout. Matthew and I are sneaking into the sound booth. We've been waiting for the perfect opportunity, and when the remaining technician gets up to go somewhere, we make our move.

"All clear, bro," Mikey says. He and Alex are on speaker phone with us, letting us know the movements of security.

"Go, go," Matthew whispers and we cut across the aisle, slip under the rope blocking off the sound booth, and climb the steps into the booth. "Where's the mic?"

"Over there." I point, and Matthew gives me a look that's both mischievous and hesitant. Then, he picks it up, and I give a little squeal. "Hello, hello—it's not on. How do I turn it on?" We both inspect the microphone, turning it over.

"Incoming, man," Alex says over speaker phone. "You've been spotted."

Matthew grabs my hand, pulling me as he fumbles with the microphone. "I got it!" he whisper-shouts. "Attention, spectators and bull riders," he says while walking toward the exit of the sound booth. "Join us at ten PM at Bryant Park for an epic snowball battle!"

"Go, go, go!" I shriek, pushing at Matthew's back. He repeats his announcement once more for good measure, then puts the microphone down and we sprint out of the booth, down the steps, and into the aisle as security spots us and starts chasing.

Alex and Mikey, still on speaker phone, are cheering through the phone. "Broooooo!" comes Mikey's voice.

We run out of the exit, the cold night air almost taking my breath away. I still hear security yelling so I'm going to keep running when Matthew tugs me behind the door, shielding me with his body as security runs right past us. I press myself into the wall and Matthew's hands cage me in on either side. Both of us are panting and smiling, trying—barely—to hold in our laughter.

After a minute, when it's clear security has breezed by us, the air shifts between us. Matthew's smile fades slowly, and I hold my breath, biting my lip as Matthew's body edges closer to mine. I reach out a tentative hand to his chest. His heart is racing under my palm, and I dare a glance at his blue eyes, and the look there is enough to stop my heart altogether. There is no question anymore in my mind—Matthew wants me just as much as I want him.

"Monica," he whispers. He leans his head against mine, his breath like a prayer on my lips.

If this wall weren't behind me holding me up, I'd be a puddle on the ground. And still, I hold back—I won't be the one to make this move. I wait patiently—okay, maybe not so patiently—for Matthew to kiss me.

He's so close, our lips must be a breath apart, when his phone—still on speaker phone, clutched in his hand right next to my head—erupts with comments from Alex and Mikey.

"Matthew? Where you at, man?"

"Did y'all get away from security? Hello?"

A small groan escapes Matthew's lips, and he shifts away from me. "Hey guys, yeah we got out. We're at the north entrance."

"Alright, we got the girls, we'll meet you there in a minute."

Matthew hangs up, and I'm hoping for us to pick off where we left off a second ago, but the moment has clearly passed. Matthew slumps against the wall next to me, tilting his head back to look at the sky. "That was pretty incredible."

"Which part? The bull riding or the sound booth escapade?"

"Both," he says with a quirk of his lips. "I've never had anyone to worry about me before," he says as his fingers reach out for mine.

"You mean, besides your mom and sister and whole family?"

He tilts his hat back, chuckling. "You know what I mean."

"Actually, I don't, Matthew Craig. Please explain." I'm teasing, but I do want him to explain. To spell it out for me.

He stands up straight and then gathers me to him, his arms linked behind my back. "I've never had someone to worry about me in a...non-platonic way." He brushes my hair over my shoulder, his fingers tracing a trail down my back. "Someone that I might want to...kiss." He says this quietly, almost a whisper. The tiniest flush of red adorns the bridge of his nose as he speaks.

"You want to kiss me, Matthew?" I bite my lip to keep myself from smiling.

He nods. "Badly."

I let myself smile—I could laugh with how giddy I am about his confession. I'm half a second away from breaking my truce with myself and standing on tiptoe to *finally* kiss this man, when I hear Katie Jo call, "Hey, lovebirds! We gotta get this celebration on the road, y'all!"

For the second time in as many minutes, Matthew groans. "We are circling back to this," he whispers to me.

"I'm counting on it," I tell him with a lingering glance that promises him I'll be counting the seconds until then.

Slay, girl.

When we get to Bryant Park, there's at least a hundred people milling around in the open space, waiting for the snowball fight. Matthew stands on a park bench, putting his fingers in his mouth to let out a whistle to get everyone's attention. "Listen up, y'all! Who wants to have a snowball fight?"

A cheer ripples through the crowd. "Then give this beautiful lady your attention, she's gonna tell you the rules." Matthew offers me a hand and I join him on the bench.

I explain the rules—no aiming at people's faces, if you're hit then you're out, and so on—and we divide everyone into two teams. Alex is leading one team, and Matthew the other. Mikey's acting as referee. "I'd destroy y'all if I played, so I'm just keepin' it fair," he'd said with a swagger.

"You'll get ten minutes to strategize and make snowballs. Once the timer goes off, the game is on!"

On Mikey's mark, the timer starts and our team runs to the far side of the clearing to strategize and make snowballs. Our crew starts packing snowballs and throwing out suggestions for the best way to defeat the other team.

"Can we get some people in the trees and get hits from overhead?" one girl suggests.

"Oh yeah, let's do it,"Matthew says. He fields suggestions and ideas from opinionated New Yorkers and cowboys like a pro, and I wonder if growing up in a family with five kids prepared him for moments like this. We strategize and make plans to defeat Alex and Mila's team, and I'm confident we'll slay.

When the timer goes off, Matthew squats in front of me, "Ready?" he says with a quirk of his mouth that looks dangerously like a smile. One I want to kiss right off his beautiful face.

"Let's put those show jumping snobs to shame," I say as I hop on his back. Matthew tilts his head back and lets out a holler. The rest of our team erupts into a war cry, and we surge forward into the clearing.

Then, the most incredible chaos happens. Snowballs are flying every which way, and I'm lobbing them from Matthew's back. We tucked snowballs into the hood of his jacket and fashioned a carrier-sling out of my scarf to carry even more. I hit one girl in the shoulder, the snow spraying all over her face as she sputters from the cold. Having the height advantage really makes a difference, and I'm able to target people before they're close enough to do anything. One guy on the opposing team clues in that there's players in the trees, and as he turns to throw a snowball up, I ping him right in the back.

"Booyah!" I shout, pointing at him.

Matthew ducks and a snowball flies right over my head, barely missing.

At this point, we're in the den of lions and our teammates are falling left and right. That's when we spot Alex and Mila—throwing snowballs back-to-back as if their very lives depend on it. I point them out to Matthew. "How many snowballs we have left?" he asks.

"Three."

He sucks in breath through his teeth. We should regroup, add more snowballs to our arsenal, but we both want to go for it. "Let's get them," he says, his voice solemn as if they'd stolen his favorite belt buckle.

Matthew charges them and I cling to his back. One guy runs up to us, arm raised to launch a ball at us, and I pump fake one of our remaining snowballs—he ducks to miss my hit, and his snowball goes flying left of us, and I still have the snowball in my hand.

As we get closer to Mila and Alex, Matthew waves down two of our comrades, instructing them to go around the other way and distract Mila and Alex. We continue to weave and dodge snowballs thrown in every direction, waiting until our teammates are in place. When we're in position, Matthew drops me gently to the ground saying, "I want in on this action." I smile, handing him a snowball.

"Let's see what you got, cowboy."

The moment Mila and Alex pivot to defend themselves, we launch our snowballs directly at their backs. They hit their targets and Matthew and I whoop, raising our hands in victory.

"Yes! Yes! Take that!" I scream at Mila and Alex. A second later, someone from the opposing team wallops us with snowballs right in my neck, getting snow all down my jacket and shirt. But we're laughing and celebrating still—our mission of getting Mila and Alex accomplished.

Matthew holds my hand as we walk to the side of the action, which is starting to dwindle as fewer players are left standing. When we're out of dodge, Matthew turns to me with the most brilliant smile on his face and says, "That was incredible. The most fun I've had in ages."

"Better than bull riding?" I ask, eyebrow raised.

He tilts his head side to side, as if deliberating. Then he pulls me into his arms, bending down to put his forehead against mine. "Bull riding is a thrill, that's for darn sure. But it's the company that makes this an even better thrill."

I burrow into his arms, enjoying the warmth after having snow down my back. "I know, Katie Jo and Mikey really make everything more fun, don't they?"

He gives a chuckle. "It's you, Monica," he says, leaning back so I can see his eyes, the warmth radiating there. "You're lighting up my world."

His words leave me speechless, so I simply smile up at him. He bends to press cold lips to my forehead. I shudder, but not just from the cold. Being close to Matthew is doing all kinds of things to my insides.

And I never want that to change.

Noche Buena

Back at my apartment, once we're dry and warm—and Matthew and I have thoroughly rubbed our win in Mila and Alex's face—the two of them announce, "We're celebrating Noche Buena!" Alex had ordered traditional Cuban and Colombian Noche Buena meals while Mila curated a playlist of songs. We eat tamales, lechón asada, arroz con moros, yuca, and, one of my favorite dessert combos: natilla and buñuelos. Together, Alex and I show the group the basic moves to dance salsa and merengue. Katie Jo jumps head first into the dancing, relentlessly teasing her brothers for their lack of 'moves.' Mikey, who can't catch on to the steps to save his life, starts creating his own dance moves, making us all laugh.

We dance and then eat and then dance some more. We all switch partners, but I make my way to Matthew more often than not. Despite confirming that he does, in fact, have one left foot and one right foot, it seems like he somehow has way more than two left feet—and yet dancing with him is the highlight of the night. The way his eyes light up when his arms are around me, or the booming laugh that escapes his lips when he misses a step...I love it.

I lose myself in this man, this moment, this memory I'm making with my friends and this newfound family.

When we're all stuffed and thoroughly worn out, we bring every pillow and blanket in the apartment out to the living room. Moving the coffee table aside, we create a warm haven in front of the couch, settling in to watch Christmas movies.

The age-old debate begins over what constitutes a Christmas classic.

"Harry Potter has a Christmas movie?" Katie Jo asks when Mila throws it out as an option.

Mila snorts, like she can't believe Katie Jo's even asking that. "Harry Potter's *classic*, KJ. *The Order of the Phoenix* is, like, the most Christmassy movie ever."

Alex and Mikey make eye contact, seeming to say, *Doubtful,* but neither of them speak up. We land on Jim Carrey's *How The Grinch Stole Christmas.* I snuggle in next to Matthew, hyper aware of every place our bodies are touching. Even through our clothes and the blankets around us, it's as if every cell in my body is focused on those places we're in contact with each other. About halfway through the movie, everyone but Matthew and I are asleep. His hand reaches for mine under the blanket, and all my nerve endings give a little cheer that I'm not asleep for this.

Who knew holding a guy's hand could be so thrilling?

But I know it's because it's not just any guy—it's Matthew.

I'm not sure how it's possible that we only met two days ago and I already feel like a changed person.

A changed person who is 100 percent falling in love with this man. I laugh quietly and shake my head—I haven't even properly kissed Matthew, and my heart is already gone for him.

A Christmas miracle straight from baby Jesus himself. He's doing a lot of those lately.

A few minutes later, when Mikey starts snoring, Matthew leans down and whispers in my ear, "Want to go somewhere?" I'm not sure how Matthew's still awake—it's after two AM and he was up early—but I have a feeling he's been biding his time the same as I have for us to catch a moment alone.

"I thought you'd never ask."

We bundle up in our coats, bringing extra blankets with us, and I lead Matthew up to the roof. Outside, the snow is falling lazily, like it's in no hurry to get to the ground. Twisting and dancing through the sky, it's mesmerizing. I've never been so entranced by snow. That is, until I hear Matthew start to play "Say You Won't Let Go" by James Arthur on his phone. He reaches out, taking my hand, and tugs me to him. "Dance with me," he says, his breath coming in little puffs in front of his face as he talks.

I fit easily into his arms, giving a little laugh when James Arthur sings about holding back his girlfriend's hair while she throws up. "Thanks for that, by the way," I tilt my head back to tell him.

A soft smile greets me as Matthew brushes my hair from my face. "I'd do it a million times over."

"Well, maybe you won't have to anymore. Unless I'm like sick-sick," I say. "I don't want to fill the voids in my life that way." I think of the pastor at church, how he talked about trying to mask his fears and insecurities with other things and it wasn't until he found God that he was truly filled. I'm beginning to see the truth in that.

Matthew cups my face, his thumb tracing my cheekbone, and I lean into him. "I'm really happy to hear that," he murmurs. "How do you feel about picking up where we left off earlier?"

I nod, standing on tiptoe to close the gap between us, but it's Matthew who leans in to brush his lips against mine.

For so much of my life, I've been seeking distraction from the bleeding holes in my heart. And every time I've had a meaningless hookup with a guy, it's given me a temporary diversion, but ultimately only served to make those holes slightly wider. But this moment is the opposite of that.

This kiss is healing. It's life. It's everything.

This man is nothing I was looking for, but everything I needed.

And this kiss...this is the kiss of a man who knows exactly what he's doing. Everything about Matthew is intentional—he doesn't do things half-hearted or halfway. He's in this for real.

I've never truly had that before, and it's equal parts intoxicating and beautiful.

Matthew and I dance and kiss, then kiss some more. After a while, we sit on a ledge, cuddling up under our blankets, and talk until dawn. I tell him about getting fired from my job, and even though it's cringy, I tell him about all the things I said to Ashton Smathers—even though he totally deserved every word, I regret it. We discuss what I could do next and options for alternative career paths. I open up to him about Eduardo and finding out his wife is pregnant, and he tells me about the wear and tear of life on the road as a bull rider. We talk about what our relationship might look like moving forward—even with so much up in the air right now, we both want this, and not just as a Christmas distraction.

For me, this is it.

It feels insane to say that after only a few days—but I've lived enough life to know forever when I see it. And with Matthew's hand in mine, forever is looking pretty good.

Cowboy Christmas

Christmas morning, we rise like the walking dead to head over to Matthew's family's rental home in Brooklyn. Mr. and Mrs. Craig, Luke, Anya, Matthew's brother John, and Mila's parents got in late last night. Their rental is a gem of a place, with an open concept and lots of funky skylights that brighten the space. Thankfully when we arrive, Mr. and Mrs. Craig and Mr. and Mrs. Kozak are still upstairs getting dressed. The brothers all gather around the dining table—a long farmhouse-style table that they're so comfortable around, it almost seems like Mrs. Craig must've imported it from home. Luke, Matthew's brother, and Anya, Mila's sister, are sitting in their wheelchairs at the corner of the table, sipping their coffee like their lives depend on it. Luke gives me a bleary eyed hello, saying, "Heard you're looking for a job. Let's talk after my second cup."

"That's your third," Anya says with her signature eye roll.

Luke shrugs as if to say, *Why bother counting?*, and goes back to sipping his coffee.

Mikey is sprawled across his chair, telling the quietest brother, John, about last night. Katie Jo is in the kitchen, scrounging around while Alex makes more coffee and Mila is slouched beside Anya, clearly not caffeinated enough yet.

I'm eyeing the table, trying to figure out where exactly I should be sitting when I first encounter Mrs. Craig—should I sit next to Mila, my best friend? Or should I sit next to Matthew, my...what is he? We talked a lot last night, but didn't get into any relationship terminology. Matthew's standing beside me, chatting with Katie Jo. They're discussing whether or not their mom will make cinnamon rolls when I notice that three of the four brothers are wearing various shades of plaid button-down shirts. "Matty," I say, ribbing him, "you didn't tell me about the plaid memo. I could've matched."

"Matty? Is she allowed to call him that?" Luke says in a mock whisper to Mikey.

"Maaaatttttyyyy," Mikey drawls it out and Matthew is quick to glare at him, his jaw ticking to tell his brothers it's most definitely not okay for anyone else to call him Matty.

I decide to go for neutral territory and sit down next to Mila, in a chair beside John, who's even more straight-faced than Matthew ever was. "You didn't tell me your little brother was even more handsome than you are," I tell Matthew, giving John a wink to let him know I'm messing around, but that seems to only make him blush, which of course only makes me want to tease him more. "I might need to trade you in for the newer model, Matthew."

At this, John's blush creeps past his cheeks all the way to his forehead.

I guess I've figured out exactly where they manufacture these guys.

"Ah, brother, don't blush," Matthew claps John's shoulders. "It'll only encourage her." Then, bending down to whisper in my ear, he says, "Give the poor kid a break. He can't handle you."

I turn toward him, our faces so close that I could kiss him if I leaned forward a hair. "Oh, but you can?" I arch a brow, enjoying his warmth.

He smirks, his breath against my ear as he says, "I think we both know the answer to that."

"Why, 'cause you're a big, bad bull-rider?"

He tilts his head, his lips twisting into a soft smile, "'Cause I'm yours."

Heat flushes through me at Matthew's whispered words, and I want to wrap my arms around him and pull him into a kiss right here, right now. But then his brothers are chattering around us, and I know we need to join in. The look that Matthew's giving me, though, tells me that we'll pick this conversation up another time.

"I always thought of myself as the most handsome of the Craig brothers," Mikey says with a waggle of his brows.

Luke snorts. "And the most humble."

"We all know who's the most attractive brother," Matthew says.

Simultaneously, Katie Jo calls out from the kitchen, "John," Mikey and Luke both say "Me," John says, "Matthew," Mila says, "Mikey."

"*Babe*," Alex says, waving his hands as if to say, *What about me?*

"Aw, honey, we're talking about the Craig brothers. You're obviously the handsomest in the room." She wraps her arms around Alex's neck and presses a kiss to his lips. I teasingly start making gagging noises at their PDA, which only serves to make Mila lean in to the kiss more.

Anya, shoulders characteristically squared, like she's sitting on a throne, sniffs and says, "It's objectively clear that Luke is the most attractive."

Luke flashes his million dollar grin and says, "Tell 'em what they already know, boss."

That's when Matthew's parents come down the stairs, and my heart rate kicks up a notch. I've never met parents before, at least, not like this. Not when I'm rapidly falling for the guy. I glance at Matthew and he gives me a reassuring smile, which only proves to make my stomach flutter.

"Ma!" Mikey calls out. "We're having a debate, you can help us. Who's the best looking of us?"

Mrs. Craig scoffs. "Katie Jo, obviously."

The guys all groan, like they should've seen this coming, but she waves them off and makes her way toward me. Her eyes—the same sea blue as Matthew's—are warm but assessing, scanning me from head to toe. "Monica, it's so nice to meet you." This woman is dripping in Southern clichés, from her overly hairsprayed locks to her plaid outfit that looks like it climbed out of the Talbots Christmas catalog.

"You too, Mrs. Craig."

"Word from the bird is that you've captured my Matthew's heart. Not that he would tell me himself." She gives her son a pointed stare.

"Ma—" Matthew starts, but she holds up a hand to silence him.

I steel myself—two years up against the bro's club at Goldman Sachs didn't make me a wimp under pressure. I meet her gaze and say, "I can't speak for Matthew's heart, Mrs. Craig, only for mine."

"And?"

I glance at Matthew, who's watching me as carefully as everyone else in the room. It's so silent, you could hear a snowflake fall.

"It's not easy to capture my heart," I start.

"Impossible," Mila chimes in.

I nod, acknowledging the truth. "But your son has done the impossible."

"I see." She presses her lips together, and I hold my breath because I have no idea what she's going to say next. This is *way* worse than the bro club. After an excruciating moment of silence, she says, "And you go to church?" She says it casually, but I understand the weight of her words.

Mila snorts, which she quickly tries to cover with a cough.

Thanks, *bestie*.

"I haven't since I was a kid. My parents' brand of Christianity didn't exactly endear me to the idea," I say with a slight grimace, "but I told Matthew I'm...changing my mind."

In the corner of my eye, Mila's jaw drops, but I hold Mrs. Craig's gaze. "Don't go just for his sake." She says it so low, I'm not sure anyone else could hear her. And, trust me, they are all trying. No one is even bothering to fake it.

"Well, to be honest, it started that way," I say, "but I think I need this more than I thought."

Mila's jaw is going to hit the ground at any moment now, but I'm speaking the truth. A God who never leaves? I can get on board with that.

"Oh, sweetheart." Mrs. Craig envelopes me in a hug that is so warm, so inviting, it feels like being cocooned in a heated blanket. And it's in this moment that I realize what Helen was saying when she fired me—it's not so much about me being *serious* as it is about me being *real*. Because I'm not usually serious, I like to have fun and make people laugh—but I can still do that while letting my walls down and letting people really see me.

Mrs. Craig's acceptance of me seems to lighten the mood, and the festivities begin with a massive breakfast that could rival any *Noche Buena* feast. We talk and laugh—all of the women want a play-by-play of the weekend while the guys pretend like they don't care. The Craig family exchanges gifts—though none of the guys give each other presents, prank or otherwise. We light the fire in the living room and Mr. Craig tells the story of Jesus's birth in a way I've never heard before. It's a little humorous and a lot magical.

I'm surprised by how at ease Matthew is around me with his family. For someone who is so buttoned up, he doesn't hesitate to hold my hand or wrap his arms around me. He makes me feel that much more at home—like I've found my place. A place I didn't even know I was missing, a place I wasn't even looking for but somehow I found. That's when I realize, it's not a place I've found—it's family.

It feels as though I've stumbled into this miracle—a Cowboy Christmas. I never in a zillion years would've thought I'd belong here, and yet, here I am. I glance up at Matthew, seeing the love, the warmth, the hope in his eyes.

My cowboy. My Matthew. My sweet distraction that turned into my forever.

Epilogue

It's been a year since that first Cowboy Christmas. A year since I met Matthew and he altered my life forever.

Well, him and baby Jesus, to be exact.

It's been a year of falling in love, getting to know Matthew better than I know anyone else—and letting myself be known as well. It's been a crazy scary ride, one that I never wanted, and yet now that I'm on it, I never want to get off.

And I'm never getting off. Today, it's official.

It's Christmas Eve and I'm waiting just inside the doors of a beautiful rooftop Manhattan venue. Could we have stayed in Florida, where all of our friends and family live? Sure. We could have. But my name (at least, for the next thirty minutes) is Monica Isabel Garcia Perez, and I don't do things in half measures. We'll have a big reception in Florida after the holidays, but this exchanging of vows couldn't be anywhere but here.

Mila stands in front of me, her eyes roving over my hair, my make-up, my dress. "You are absolute perfection, *chica bonita*," she says in her *gringa* voice and I laugh. I throw my arms around her and squeeze her tight, then place my hands on her belly with its own little

Christmas miracle. Mila glances down at my hands, then back at me, and tears sprout in her eyes.

"Stupid hormones," she says, wiping her eyes. "I'll be right back."

Katie Jo and Mama Craig—what she insists on me calling her—walk up to hug me and kiss my cheek. "You're gonna be my sister!" Katie Jo crows.

"We're doing the best we can to balance out all that testosterone in this family," Mama Craig says with a grin, but then she sobers, cupping my cheek with her hand. "You are a wonderful addition to our family, Monica."

"Thank you," I tell her, trying to blink the tears away. "Hey, now that I'm joining the family, do I get to learn the story behind Prankmas?" I ask, referring to the mysterious Christmas prank shenanigans that forced Mrs. Craig to call off any gift-giving between the brothers. Of course, she made one exception for Matthew's wedding gift from the brothers—as long as she got to approve it before it was given. (The gift is not mysterious: it was a Trager Outlaw 885 Pellet Grill. For all the other city girls like me reading this...it's basically a big, fancy barbecue contraption.)

Mrs. Craig pats my cheek and withdraws her hand. "What are the kids saying these days? IYKYK?" *If you know, you know.* She winks at me as the event planner calls for her, and she turns away. "See you out there, sweetheart."

I frown at her back, wondering, *did she really just turn me down?* Will I ever find out about Prankmas?

"Don't worry, sugar," Katie Jo says, "I'll tell you all the other family secrets."

I raise an eyebrow. "Just not that one?"

"Sworn to secrecy. But maybe you can get it out of Matthew. A little pillow talk, y'know?" she waggles her blonde eyebrows and I laugh, shaking my head. "Time to go," she says, blowing me a kiss as she walks out the door.

A few moments later, Mila's back and she's squeezing my hand. "You ready?" she asks.

I nod, feeling wobbly on my feet and yet, somehow, also very steady.

"He's the one in the cowboy hat," she says over her shoulder. "In case you get confused."

I laugh, rolling my eyes. "Thanks, Milly Vanilly."

Then, she's gone and I'm left to wait some more. My parents quietly approach from behind, putting their arms around me. "*Lista, hija?*" my mom asks. I nod, taking her hand as I attempt to breathe deeply. My gorgeous designer dress isn't exactly helping, but it's *so* worth it.

Since I moved back to South Florida and started managing Luke's wheelchair company, Wheelz, my parents and I have worked through our fair share of challenges. It took a few months of counseling to be able to talk with them about how their abandonment affected me—not only as a child, but now as an adult. The wounds are still there, but they're healing. Slowly but surely. And Matthew's been there by my side through it all. A few months ago, he came off the bull riding circuit, claiming he's 'too old' to get bucked off every night. He's now the barn manager at Mila's rapidly expanding equine-assisted therapy center and it could not be a better fit for him.

The event planner pokes her head through the door and tells us it's time. My parents each take an arm, and together we walk out into the cold winter air. Space heaters dot the roof, keeping our guests in relative warmth. Snow is falling, creating a magical, snowglobe-effect on the scenery. The darkening city stretches in every direction around us. Twinkle lights strung overhead give the venue a glow, and each guest is holding an LED candle as I walk down the aisle.

When I see Matthew—sure enough, wearing a pristine white cowboy hat—I let the tears fall, even though it's messing up my makeup. I don't care. I'd rather be immortalized in our wedding photos as a teary-eyed mess than a made-up mannequin. I may be a lot of things, but at least now I'm *real*.

Matthew's smile beckons me forward, and even though I pass family and friends, I see none of them. He's the only one who exists, the only one I have eyes for.

When I finally reach him, he tucks my hands in between his, warming me. "Fancy meetin' you here," he says with a wink.

I should think of a witty reply, but I can't. I'm just so wrapped up in this man, this moment, that I lose myself in him for a little while. Mr. Craig—Pastor Craig, I should say—is performing our wedding. He recounts some of the funnier—and more crowd-appropriate—parts of our first weekend together, and Matthew and I laugh at his retelling. Mr. Craig is a born storyteller, and I love that about him.

It still shocks me to think about how hard and fast I fell for Matthew—and, possibly more surprising, how fast *he* fell for *me*—but the more I think about it, the more I'm convinced that God had been preparing me for Matthew my whole life. This is exactly how it was supposed to happen.

When Mr. Craig has Matthew kiss his bride—that's *me!*—at long last, I fall into his kiss. Matthew's kiss is everything that embodies him—it's quiet at first, then passionate and warm. It's intentional and full. It's honest and real. It's beautiful and everything a woman could ever hope for.

Matthew is my last first kiss, and I wouldn't have it any other way. He's the distraction I wanted, the husband I never thought I deserved, all wrapped up in this beautiful man who swept me off my feet and made all my walls come crashing down.

My wonderful Christmas cowboy.

If you enjoyed this book, would you consider leaving a review? Reviews are the lifeblood of books and authors. Please support this Indie author by reviewing this book here:

REVIEW THE COWBOY CHRISTMAS DISTRACTION

Scan the QR codes or go to the links below to leave a review.

Goodreads:

https://tinyurl.com/ ccdreview1

Amazon:

https://tinyurl.com/ ccdreview2

Keep reading for excerpts from Tiffany's other novels!

Also by Tiffany

Equestrian Dreams: A Florida Sweet Romance Series:
Off Course (#0.5)
JUMP (#1)
FALL (#2)
SOAR (#3) – coming February 2024

Keep reading for an excerpt from the free prequel novella for the Equestrian Dreams series...

Off Course: An Excerpt

Alex

It's pathetic, I know. I look for almost any reason to be around her. Is it wrong? Maybe. She's got a boyfriend. Does it make me feel better? Nope. It's like a stab in the gut every time I remember she's taken. But can I stop? Also, no.

So when Mila shows up to the barn for her lesson, I'm here to help her with Ozzy. I know she gets lessons on Tuesdays, so I try to get done whatever I need to before she comes so I'm available.

It's pitiful, I know.

But when Mila asks if I'm dating anyone, I wonder if maybe it's all been worth it. Her question surprises me, and like the dolt that I am, I freeze mid-curry, my brain unable to process why she'd ask me this. Of course the first thing that pops into my mind is that she and Michael broke up and she's putting feelers out, but I immediately chastise myself for my wishful thinking.

"I'm sorry if that was inappropriate of me to ask," she says before I can respond, and the bashful look on her face is so adorable, it makes my heart squeeze.

"No, not at all. I'm just...surprised, that's all." I get the words out, barely, and return dutifully to the task at hand, focusing on currying Ozzy so that I don't have to look at Mila anymore and potentially give away how much hope is throbbing through my chest right now.

"Are you, y'know, open?" she asks, lighthearted and casual.

"To dating?" I'm still trying to gauge her intentions. Mila's so confident, she'd have no problem whatsoever asking a guy out—but would she ask *me* out? I'm not so sure. Michael and I could not be more different. But a guy can hope, can't he?

She nods, and I find myself falling into her hazel eyes.

"Yes," I say, keeping my gaze steady on hers. How many times have I dreamed of something—anything—happening with Mila? Is it even possible that it's happening right now? I have to know, though, what's really going on, so I say, "I thought...isn't, um." I look away. "Aren't you...with, you know, Michael?"

I force myself to look her in the eye again, and that's when I see it—she definitely was *not* asking me out. "I—yes, we're still going out. I was thinking of setting up like a double date with my sister," she stammers.

You idiot, I berate myself. I let my hope get the best of me—my fanciful thinking that one day Mila will come to her senses and see that I'm the right guy for her—and it's going to be my ruin. "A date with Anya?" I attempt to sound casual, like I didn't just make a fool of myself.

She nods again, and I can tell she sees right through me. It cuts me down and I feel like I'm three feet tall. I toss the curry comb into the grooming box and grab the body brush, thankful that at least we have a horse between us. To shield me just a little.

I think about what Mila's saying—she wants me to take Anya on a date? I try to tell myself this is a good thing. Anya is beautiful, talented, smart. She's a catch by anyone's standards. And Mila obviously thinks I'm good enough to take her sister out. I just wish she thought I was good enough to take *her* out. I consider for a second taking Anya out.

But I couldn't do it—not to myself, not to Anya—knowing that the whole time I'd just be wishing it were Mila. It wouldn't be fair to Anya, or myself. "I can't take Anya on a date. Sorry, Mila. I could ask someone else, though. Maybe Ryan could take her out?"

I know Anya would never go out with Ryan—she can't help but roll her eyes every time he shows up—but I needed to say *something*, offer some sort of solution.

"Sure, yeah, that would be nice," Mila says, but her words aren't very convincing. She's disappointed, and I hate disappointing her. But I also know I did the right thing.

We tack up Ozzy in silence, falling into a rhythm with each other that, for me, is noteworthy. We work well together. We anticipate each other's movements, not having to ask for the girth or the bridle, it just happens, as if we're synced on some metaphysical level.

When I give her a leg-up, she glances back down at me, our eyes locking, lingering for a few seconds. I soak it in, wanting so much more than this, but content with a little piece of her attention.

It's pathetic, I know. But I keep holding out hope that one day, she'll give me a chance.

Download Off Course for free to follow Mila and Alex's love story!

OFF COURSE:
A Prequel Novella

Scan the QR code or go to the
link below to download the
FREE prequel novella for the
Equestrian Dreams series.

tinyurl.com/offcoursebook

Jump: An Excerpt

Mila

Prior to this scene, Mila's boyfriend, Michael, broke up with her a few weeks ago. She just got off the phone with her dad, who is pressuring her to get her grad school applications done.

We hang up, and instead of working on my application essay, I shut my laptop defiantly and hop in the shower. I listen to my Breakup playlist, belting the lines from Ashe and Niall Horan's song "Moral of the Story." When the song ends, I reach out of the shower and replay it. As I sing along, I want to tell Ashe I'm in pain *and* still in love. The problem is, I don't want to *not* be in love—I just want to be out of pain. When Ariana Grande's "thank u, next" comes on, I try to muster her confidence, and fail.

Out of the shower, I pull up *National Velvet* for the zillionth time. As I watch a young Elizabeth Taylor pretending to gallop down the pathway to her house, I scroll through my text thread with Michael.

All of our texts are pre-Breakup. Lovely texts, sweet texts. Rest-of-my-life texts.

Just last week he'd sent me a picture of the sunset at the barn and said: *Wish you were here with me, you'd make the view 10000x better.*

I don't get it. We had everything—everything a couple could possibly want—and he just threw it away with both hands as if it were nothing. I text my best friend and old dorm roomie, Monica: *I need you to make sure I don't text Michael right now.*

I open my photos and flip through shots from the early days of our relationship. There's a blurry one from Kickback Tavern, our barn's go-to Sunday night restaurant haunt. Michael and me with our faces smooshed together, a cover band somewhere in the background. One at WEF with Michael's bay horse, Khan, in between us. I pause at a photo of us on my birthday last year when Michael took me on a helicopter ride and then dinner at a rooftop terrace with a private chef. It was incredible, one of the best nights of my life, until the very end of the night when it was soured by a shocking revelation that I can't even bring myself to think about. But when I look at the picture, with Michael in his slick Tom Ford suit and me in Anya's hot pink Monique Lhuillier dress, it's like nothing bad ever happened that night. Isn't that funny, how memories can either grow in their bitterness, or all the bad things slough off until you're left with a hazy, happy memory where nothing went wrong?

The nostalgia builds until I open up my text thread with Michael (of course Monica hasn't texted me back, so what else am I supposed to do?) and start to text him. First, an *I miss you*—but that feels too desperate, so I erase it. Then, just a *hey* but that's too nonchalant. I type and subsequently erase several more options, ranging from over-sharing (a long diatribe about my day) to sappy (*I've only ever loved you*) to petty (*Hey Greg! Had so much fun with you last night. Looking forward to Friday.*). Next I went with humorous: *Booty call??*

I'm laughing at myself as I erase that option when the three dots pop up that indicate Michael is typing something. I sit up quickly, gripping the phone in my hand, my eyes wide as I watch the dots appear, then disappear. My heart hammers against my chest, threatening to force its way through. I scramble for the remote, pausing the movie.

This needs my full attention.

Was he missing me, too? Did he regret The Breakup?

I watch the text thread so closely, I'm sure Michael can feel me staring through the screen.

"C'mon, c'mon, c'mon," I mumble, shaking my phone.

I shake the phone so hard, the 'redo typing' message pops up—except I think it says, 'undo typing.' With tremoring hands, I click the 'redo' button—which I *think* is the 'undo' button—and my previous *Booty call??* text comes back onto the screen. In my haste to re-erase it, I click send.

"NO! NO! NO!" I scream at my phone while I try in vain to undo the message, managing instead to heart the text. I fumble with my phone, trying to fix my mistake, but there's nothing I can do except un-heart the message. I stare at it, gaping at the screen, my pulse is so hard and fast, it feels like my carotid artery might strangle me. In an outburst of frustration, I throw my phone to the floor and pace around my room, raking my hands through my hair as I try to figure out what in the world I can do.

The panic I feel is suffocating. My chest is tight with fear for what seems like the fifteenth time that day. When will it end? When will I feel like a normal person again? I want so badly to cry—to just let it all out—but the tears don't come, and that only makes me more distraught. Like I'm stuck behind the walls of my emotions and they won't let me out.

This isn't the sort of text a girl like me would send. Not in a million years, not if someone held a gun to my head and told me to send this text. (Okay, *maybe* in that particular instance I would send the text. But you get the idea.)

I know I need to figure out a solution. Do I call him and tell him it was a joke? That I didn't mean to send it? Or does that just make me look more desperate?

What if he responds with mockery or vitriol? I would die. I would literally melt into a puddle of steaming hot liquid embarrassment and cease to exist from sheer shame.

My heart does a double-beat as I think of another option: what if he responds positively to my ridiculous text? And that somehow leads to us getting back together?

My hands shake with the idea. I clamber to my phone and pick it up.

No response.

"Ugh!" I shake the phone again, and of course the 'undo typing' message pops up and I scream at my phone again. "Stop! Stop!"

In utter defeat, I turn off my phone and climb in bed, too agitated to watch *National Velvet* anymore. With limited options, I get back out of bed and go through a body weight cardio circuit—jumping jacks, burpees, mountain climbers. Then three minute-long planks, counting to myself, until my arms and core are quivering.

I hide under my obnoxiously cheerful quilt and turn my phone back on, daring to peek at the text thread with Michael again, but there's nothing except a text from Monica: *Stay strong, Mila!* along with a GIF of a female bodybuilder undulating her chest muscles. Any other time, I'd think this was hilarious. But not today. I close my eyes, burying my head in my arms, wondering if I'll need to stay hidden here forever.

Eventually I go back to *National Velvet*, and fall asleep sometime after two in the morning, only to have my normal round of nightmares. Except this time Michael is on the sidelines laughing at me.

Buy JUMP and find out what happens to Mila!

JUMP:
Equestrian Dreams Book One

Scan the QR code or go to the
link below to purchase JUMP.

https://tinyurl.com/thejumpbook

Acknowledgements

First and foremost: I'm so grateful to the God who never leaves. Every good thing truly comes from You.

My husband, Tyler, has inspired and supported my writing at every turn, and I'm so grateful. I may technically dedicate books to other people, but they're all for you. Thanks for making it easy to write swoonworthy guys. (I know you're going to hate that word 'swoonworthy' but there it is. I love you.)

My sister-in-law, Amanda, who has the unfortunate task of reading all of my worst drafts: Thank you, thank you, thank you. I'm so thankful for you. If we were picking snowball fight teams, I'd choose you (though we'd probably lose since we're both Florida girls. But at least we'd lose together!).

To my family: Mom, Dad, Jeff, Lisa, Joey, Philippa, Kyle, Amanda, Daniel, Ryan, Andrea, Scotty and Dorothy. Thank you for all your endless support! I love writing big family scenes (like at the end of this book) because of our big, wonderful, crazy family (okay, maybe it's just the Stearns side that's crazy, but still). You are all amazing and I'm so grateful for your love and encouragement.

My brother, Daniel, is an incredible filmmaker and he created a book trailer for my first novel, JUMP, that is amazing. Thank you, thank you, thank you. Many thanks to Nora Pantoja and Gabriel Jose

Bonilla who played Mila and Alex. Y'all are so talented and I'm blessed to have worked with you. (Also, if you haven't seen the trailer, check it out in the QR code below. And follow Daniel's filmmaking projects on Instagram @daniel.filmmaking. You won't regret it.)

Joyce Bloemker, editor extraordinaire, gave me valuable feedback as an editor. If you are a writer in need of an editor, definitely look up Joyce (who also happens to be a horse person!). You can find her on Instagram @palomino.and.pinto.

Jesi Colston has been a wonderful friend who has supported me in multiple ways, including bringing copies of my books on vacation with her to put in little free libraries around the world! Thank you, my friend!

Thanks to everyone who was an ARC reader and who joined my launch team for this book and any other, thank you for your ongoing support! It's readers like you who keep us Indie authors going! You're awesome and so fun!

Infinite thanks to Lauren, our babysitter, without whom this book would not have been written. I love and appreciate your enthusiasm for my boys.

To all of the bloggers, podcasters, bookstagrammers, BookTokers and others who helped spread the word about JUMP, FALL, and now CCD: thank you thank you thank you!! You are the lifeblood of this industry and I'm grateful for you. Special thanks to Rachel @closeddoorromance who has curated a massive database of clean or 'closed door' romance authors and does so much for Indie authors.

To all who left reviews and spread the word about my books, you have no idea how much that means to me. You are helping my books to find their way into the hands and devices of its ideal readers. Thank you!!!

And thank you, dear reader, for continuing this journey with me and making this dream a reality.

Want to connect? I have a Facebook reader group where I give updates, let you vote on things like character names and book cover designs, and post teasers and bonus content! Join here:

VIEW THE JUMP TRAILER HERE:

Scan the QR code or go to the link below to see the JUMP trailer:

https://tinyurl.com/jumptrailer

About the Author

As a Florida girl, Tiffany would probably freeze to death in a New York City winter. A horse girl through and through, she's been riding horses since before she could walk. She's a five-time IAHA national champion and competed regularly at the Winter Equestrian Festival with her gentle giant, Obi-Wan. She received her Masters of Fine Arts in Creative Writing from the University of Tampa. She lives in Tampa with her middle-school sweetheart and her two wild and crazy sons. You can follow her on TikTok, Instagram and Facebook @tiffanynoellechacon or on her website at tiffanynoellechacon.com.